UNTIL THE DAY ARRIVES

UNTIL THE DAY ARRIVES

ANA MARIA MACHADO

TRANSLATED BY JANE SPRINGER

Groundwood Books
House of Anansi Press
Toronto / Berkeley

Groundwood Books / House of Anansi Press
110 Spadina Avenue, Suite 801, Toronto, Ontario M5V 2K4
or c/o Publishers Group West
1700 Fourth Street, Berkeley, CA 94710

We acknowledge for their financial support of our publishing program
the Government of Canada through the Canada Book Fund (CBF).

Library and Archives Canada Cataloguing in Publication
Machado, Ana Maria
[Enquanto o dia não chega. English]
Until the day arrives / written by Ana Maria Machado ; translated by Jane Springer.
Translation of: Enquanto o dia não chega.
Issued in print and electronic formats.
ISBN 978-1-55498-455-8 (bound).—ISBN 978-1-55498-457-2 (html)
I. Springer, Jane, translator II. Title. III. Title: Enquanto o dia não chega. English.
PZ7.M1795Un 2014   j869.3'42   C2014-901609-3
C2014-901610-7

Cover illustration by Richard Rudnicki
Design by Michael Solomon

Groundwood Books is committed to protecting our natural environment.
As part of our efforts, the interior of this book is printed on paper that contains 100%
post-consumer recycled fibers, is acid-free and is processed chlorine-free.

Printed and bound in Canada

Contents

1

___

Bento

IT WAS ALL very unexpected. All it took was an instant. In a few minutes, Bento's life changed forever. And Manu's life, too, although it wasn't obvious at the time.

Manu saw the guards take Bento away. But all he could do was hide so as not to be seized as well.

It wasn't clear how the brawl had started. But it soon became violent, ugly. Manu heard the shouting and saw Bento throw a plate of leftover food at someone. There was such an uproar that it was impossible to make out what was going on. He wanted to help, but he was too far away, coming down the stairs with a tray that the tavern's owner had asked him to bring from one of the rooms.

Bottles were flying, barrels were rolling, dishes were breaking, creating a huge din. Some of the brawlers joined arms to overturn the heavy, long table that would seat ten men at the end of the day. In seconds, it was transformed into a barricade, protecting Bento and the innkeeper's son.

"Call the king's guards!" someone shouted.

Everyone in the city knew that this distress call would soon bring the soldiers of the king. They'd arrive in no time, aggressive and confrontational.

Manu stood on the stairs, tray in hand, stunned by the sudden violence. Bento signaled not to go down. Without actually hearing his words, Manu understood perfectly what he was saying, his hands cupped around his mouth.

"Get out of here! Don't let them grab you!"

Manu stepped back and hid behind a huge chest on the landing that was used for storing mugs and tin plates. Afraid and angry at the same time, he wanted to run away and disappear, but also felt like jumping into the fray and swatting people left and right, or smashing someone with the tray. He didn't know what to do, but obeyed Bento. His heart was pounding hard enough to burst.

From his hiding place he watched as someone evil-looking hit Bento on the head with a heavy object. A candlestick, maybe. Bento staggered. A trickle of blood began to drip down his forehead.

"Here come the guards! The guards!"

As the message spread, people ran in all directions. The place emptied in seconds. Only Bento was left standing in the immense room, half-dazed, disoriented, not really seeing straight. He swung and lumbered all over the place, and then he fell. Three pairs of arms grabbed him at the same time. They all belonged to soldiers of the guard.

He tried hard to defend himself.

"Let go of me! I didn't do anything! Hurry, go after them! The guilty ones are going to escape!"

Bento was given a huge shove, while the soldier who seemed to be in charge answered him.

"What guilty ones? There's nobody else here. Only you, and you're going to stay tied up while the innkeeper serves us a good wine to thank us for restoring order."

That was too much. Already angry, Bento became furious.

"There's no one here because everyone has fled. Are you going to let them escape? Run after them! Hurry up, you cowards!"

One of the soldiers drew his sword menacingly. Two others bound Bento's wrists with a rope and forced him to sit on the stairs. But this still didn't silence the boy. Bloodied and angry, he continued to fight with words.

"Surely His Majesty doesn't pay your wages so you can sip wine for free instead of chasing hoodlums!"

"We're holding the only troublemaker we found — a troublemaker who can barely stand up he's been drinking so much. Not to mention he's nearly destroyed the workplace that supports a family. And now he's incurred new crimes — disregarding the guards' authority and even managing to insult His Majesty."

Bento knew better than to continue to rant. It would only complicate his situation. It was better to remain silent.

Stammering with fear, the tavern owner tried to explain what had happened.

"He's ri-i-i-ight, sirs. He's t-t-telling the t-t-truth …"

The guard commander's response was sharp.

"Don't argue, man! Bring us our wine, right away. Or do you want us to take you in, too?"

Even though he was Bento's boss, the innkeeper knew that he was helpless against this brutality. There was no use trying to explain anything.

Quietly sitting on the step, his wrists tied, his head aching and bleeding, Bento was beginning to understand the full extent of the danger he was in. But gripped by an older brother's concern, he remembered his father's advice. He was responsible. He couldn't let anything bad happen to Manu.

Careful not to turn his head, he looked through the wooden banister and spotted the small figure crouching behind the chest. He did what he could. Pretending to scratch his face, he raised his tied hands and held his right index finger in front of his mouth. It was an eloquent plea for silence. A silent piece of brotherly advice and protection.

His guidance was understood and followed. Wavering between wanting to run off and a rash desire to attack the guards, the hidden figure shrank a little into the shadows. It was from there that Manu watched the soldiers take Bento away. Where, he didn't know, but he would find out. Even if it meant searching all over Lisbon.

2

Manu

MANU WAS EXHAUSTED and hungry — very hungry. A little cold, too. He needed to get something to eat and find a place to spend the night that was sheltered from the wind.

The past few days had been difficult, the day before particularly upsetting. Things had improved when Manu came to Lisbon with Bento, but recently everything had turned bad again. Very bad.

At first, right after the fight and Bento's arrest, Manu managed to stay at the tavern, working hard — helping to serve tables, carrying water, washing dishes, sweeping the floor. In return, he had enough to eat and a place to sleep. There was more work now that Bento wasn't there. The innkeeper and his wife agreed to let Manu continue because they needed help, even if it was a child's help.

"A kid's work is only a trifle, but anyone who doesn't

take advantage of it is crazy," the boss would always say.

And his wife would sometimes acknowledge in a protective tone, "The kid works hard."

The nickname stuck. It was kid here, kid there. No one was interested in knowing his real name.

"Kid, go fetch a pail of water from the well there."

"Take this to that table, kid. But be careful, it's hot!"

Heavy or not, Manu carried it, taking small steps, sometimes stumbling. He did what was possible, being slight and not yet twelve. The child followed every order, more than ever now that Bento was gone.

Desperate to find out where Bento was, Manu struggled to overhear conversations while serving tables. But the subject never came up. No one seemed to remember what had happened. Finally, Manu drummed up the courage to ask the innkeeper's wife.

"Where did they take my brother?"

"To jail, of course. Where did you think he would be? He's probably been flung into a dungeon by now."

This was very vague. Manu persisted.

"And where is this dungeon?"

"I don't know."

"How can we find out?"

The woman looked admiringly at the dirty little face, with its delicate lines and bright, curious expression.

"I have no idea, but I can ask my husband."

And she continued to scald the freshly slaughtered chicken she was using to prepare soup.

A while later, when the innkeeper came into the kitchen, Manu reminded her, "Don't forget to ask him, please?"

"Ask what?"

"Where the dungeon is ..."

The woman turned to look at the child and took pity. She faced her husband.

"Tavares, do you know where they took Bento?"

"To prison, of course."

Manu could not help asking, "Where is this prison? And what will they do with him?"

"I don't know. You never know. But there's usually a stiff penalty in such cases. It wasn't just a fight — he's accused of insulting the king."

"That's not true," Manu protested. "We all know that it isn't true."

"You think you can convince the guards? The judges?" said the man, smiling.

"I don't know. But I can go there and explain what happened."

The innkeepers laughed, thinking that kids just didn't understand how the world worked. Just imagine, a child being allowed to enter a prison or a court and arguing with the authorities.

But Manu insisted, "Where is this prison? Where did they take Bento?"

The innkeeper carefully explained how to get to the gates of the building where he supposed the boy was locked up. But he added, "Don't get into any more trouble. If you even go near there, don't bother coming back. I don't want those guards in my house again."

And that's how Manu lost his job. He took the boss's words quite literally. Of course he went to the prison to try to rescue Bento — and afterwards never returned to the inn.

The rescue attempt was futile. Nobody could be bothered to listen to Manu, and they didn't let him into the prison. It wasn't even possible to find someone trustworthy to give Bento their father's pocket knife. He might need it, being alone inside the dungeon.

Now Manu was wandering the hills of Lisbon, having eaten nothing for two days except a scrap of old bread a woman had given him the day before. His belly rumbled, his head ached and his vision was a little cloudy. Hunger seemed to make everything colder. Dark clouds were gathering in the sky, threatening rain, and thunder became increasingly frequent. The wind was icy with heavy moisture from the river, cutting Manu's skin. He needed to find some shelter.

Turning a corner, Manu saw four or five people sitting on the side steps of a church. They were dressed in very old, worn clothes, some of them in rags. As he approached, the door of the sacristy opened. Everyone stood up.

"Did you also come for the soup?" asked the sexton.

"Yes," Manu affirmed, hearing about the food.

"Every day there's a new mouth," was the response.

The sexton offered him a slice of bread and a bowl of hot liquid with chunks of cabbage and turnip floating in it. Manu ate heartily. When he returned the bowl, he asked the sexton if he could help with something in return for the meal. He offered to wash dishes or carry water.

"So take this bucket and bring me some water," the man accepted, barely glancing in Manu's direction. With a nod, he indicated a well that could be seen through a half-open door. It was in the inner courtyard of the cloister — a small garden, with orange trees and medicinal herbs, surrounded by galleries with archways that were supported by finely carved stone columns.

During his little foray into the courtyard, Manu noticed another partly open door that led into the church. It would be a sheltered place to spend the night, he thought. Leaving the bucket in the sacristy, he took advantage of the sexton looking the other way to slip inside.

It was a huge stone church, with an elevated nave full of columns. Perhaps during the day, when the sun was shining, some light seeped through the stained-glass windows way up there, close to the ceiling. But at that time, as the sun was going down, the church was very dark and a little daunting in its magnitude and solemnity. It resembled a large cave where wolves and bears would live. Everywhere, there were strange and menacing carved stone figures that seemed to have walked out of a nightmare. The church was frightening. But it was the house of God, Manu knew. And there was no rain or wind.

After a while, Manu heard the sexton's footsteps. He drew back and ducked behind a low wall, then climbed a small spiral staircase and hid in the pulpit.

There was no need to worry. The man didn't enter the church. He had just come to close the heavy door, which creaked loudly. He didn't even glance inside. It didn't enter his head that a child could be hiding within those walls.

And so Manu started sleeping in the house of God. It was cold, but it was protected from the elements, including the sudden bursts of lightning, which on that first night flashed through the windows, illuminating the stone figures and casting colorful shadows in ghostly corners.

Besides being a sheltered place, the church brought the prospect of hot broth every night. It also secured what may have been Manu's only solace — the loving smile of a stone lady with a small boy on her lap. Our Lady, everyone said. Manu knew who she was and remembered how their mother used to pray to her, saying a Hail Mary with each bead of the rosary. Before their mother died, she had feebly asked the mother of Jesus to take care of her children who would be alone in the world.

That first night in the church — listening to the storm outside and wondering how to find Bento — Manu felt protected. He settled down to sleep at the top of some steps, right at the foot of Mary's altar. Close by were the stubs of lit candles. In the weak and trembling light, Manu could see the strength in that maternal figure. It was as if his mother were still there, pushing sadness a little farther away and making him feel a little less alone.

3

Alone

MANU SPENT a few days wandering around the town and sleeping in the church at night, after doing dishes, carrying wood and fetching water for the sexton. There had been no contact with Bento. Manu had no idea how to get him out of prison. Force wasn't an option, since Manu was weak and without resources. Tears and appeals were not going to work, either. Manu had already cried and begged in front of the guards, but was met only with cruelty, laughter and ridicule.

"Here comes the whiner again."

"Get out of here, kid!"

"Nuisance!"

He hovered around like a silly, sluggish fly that insists on landing everywhere, until finally he would scarcely show up before the guards tried to get rid of him. They wouldn't even let him linger near the gates as they had in the early days.

If only Manu could talk to Bento, surely he would be able to come up with a plan. His older brother was smart and full of ideas. If it hadn't been for him, the two of them would still be in the village where they were born. Or they would have died of the plague, like the rest of their family and almost all their neighbors.

Just thinking about it made Manu's eyes cloud up and almost overflow with tears. His head and heart were filled with sad memories of two younger brothers and their mother and father. They had all been sick in the small, dark house, and when they stopped clinging to life, their bodies were thrown on top of the pile that was growing at the front door. Then, one by one, they were taken away in the wagon used to carry the dead. It was done in a hurry, because there were so many bodies, and burials had to be quick to try to contain the plague that raged from street to street.

Manu would never forget the day they put their father's body on the wagon, and the two of them were all alone. Bento made a decision.

"Father told me to look after you and take care of everything. Let's get out of here."

"Where should we go?"

"I don't know. But staying means waiting for the plague to get us, too. We have to get away, right now. The whole town is sick, Manu. It's only a matter of time."

Time — trying to escape time. Moving away from an earlier time — a wonderful time, with family, their siblings' playfulness, their mother's lap and smile, their father's voice telling stories by the fire at the end of the day. The time when Manu had a home.

All this had been left behind.

Within hours, they were on the road. They took only a few things — a change of clothes from one sibling, a coat inherited from another, their mother's rosary, their father's pocket knife. And a small object — the ceramic dove that Manu quickly snatched from a shelf and tucked in a pocket just before they left. It was so tiny and delicate, white and blue. Manu didn't know if it was a toy or an ornament.

He remembered when it had been made. Their father had brought home a ball of clay from the workshop. It was wrapped in a damp cloth, and he showed the children how to shape it. All of them spent a Sunday playing with the clay, making models of animals — roosters, dogs and cats. None was as beautiful or as perfect as the small dove that emerged from their father's deft fingers while he was teaching them. Manu would never forget their father's long, magical hands, which were able to give life to wet earth.

The next day, Manu went with him to the workshop. Taking advantage of the hot kiln used to fire the dishes made by the pottery workers, he put the clay dove inside to fix the glaze. Manu saw how he had painted the dove with pigments that would change color with the heat of the kiln and turn the scratched lines representing the dove's feathers blue. Later, when it came time to take everything out of the kiln, there it was amid all the pots and jars — a graceful blue-and-white glazed dove, tiny and perfect, ready to go back to their home. The dove lived on the shelf, looking as if it had just softly landed there to celebrate a day of peace and family joy. It watched over them all.

But the dove belonged to Manu. Forever after, he would remember the smile with which their father handed him the dove when it had cooled.

"Take it," he said. "It's for you." And he patted Manu on the head with his long fingers.

"I also want to work in a pottery when I grow up."

"Well, I'll teach you some secrets, so that when you are apprenticing you'll know a thing or two."

And that's how Manu started going to work with their father. First, Manu helped him with ceramic tiles, which were easy to make because they were square and had ready-made molds that were assembled on a trivet to go into the kiln. But little by little, Manu tried other things. Playing with the clay was fun. So was shaping it into long, thin pieces that would become the handles of mugs or pitchers.

More than anything, Manu wanted to master the potter's wheel, where your feet turned a platform on which you put the wet mass. There your hands formed a roundness out of the clay, leaving a hollow at its core, creating pitchers, candlesticks, vases, bowls, pots of all kinds. But it was hard to do with small fingers, and Manu wondered whether it would ever be possible to learn how to do it well. In spite of this, their father encouraged him to keep trying.

"This is the way your hands become used to the wheel," he said. "It's a matter of feeling and being familiar with it. Absorb it little by little and you'll find that you won't ever forget."

Manu didn't forget.

What Manu couldn't have imagined is that shortly afterwards there would be no father to continue the teaching, nor a mother waiting at home with food ready on the table. Nor could Manu have imagined being on the road with Bento, every day a little farther from the place where they were born and the cemetery where they had buried the rest of their family.

Manu and Bento were the only ones left.

Each day they traveled until they could go no farther. They drank water from streams and ate fruit from trees along the way. They slept in fields, on the hard ground. And the next day they kept walking. They kept going farther and farther from home, and, they hoped, from death.

They offered to help with odd jobs on the farms and in the villages they passed through in exchange for a meal and a night sleeping in a barn or on a pile of straw. Sometimes a farmer would give them a ride on a hay wagon carting casks of wine or olive oil to a nearby market.

After a few weeks, they made it to Lisbon, tired but still alive. It was a day of celebration, with processions and singing, but they were dusty, spattered with mud and poorly dressed. It was then that Bento had the idea to go to the tavern in search of work.

When they arrived, they were both clean and tidy, having bathed in the fountain in the square. Their hair was newly cut with the pocket knife, and they were wearing clean clothes they had brought from home. The clothes may not have been exactly the right size, but they were fresh and in good condition and weren't covered with road dust.

That was only a few months ago, but it seemed like years. They had left their family, their home, their freedom — everything — behind. Even Bento was gone now. And without Bento, Manu had no idea what to do. He was all on his own, looking for shelter.

And he was hungry. How could anyone think when their stomach was growling? The soup from the church barely warmed him or lasted him through the night. At dawn, it was a little less chilly, but Manu couldn't worry about being hungry then. The sexton would open the main door of the church, and people would begin to arrive for mass. Manu had to go out and walk in the sun and start to warm up. But soon that miserable feeling was back. The sense of emptiness just got worse. A hollow pain. Hunger.

Manu spent the whole day walking aimlessly through the market stalls, waiting for some leftover food to fall to the ground, or hoping to nibble on a discarded fruit or vegetable that was not totally spoiled. But a lot of other people had the same idea. Manu had to compete for the scraps with beggars of all kinds. Even dogs were on the prowl for a bone to gnaw or a piece of sausage to snatch, as they circled through the legs of the customers and vendors.

A little ahead of Manu, in the shadow of a small awning, was a table full of carefully displayed fruit. He thought of passing by surreptitiously, like someone distracted, and grabbing some. It was important to plan what to take. A few berries wouldn't help much. But a melon would certainly soothe the stomach. But what if the owner saw, or if that perfectly balanced stack collapsed all at once and all those colorful fruits tumbled to the ground? There would be a chase, a huge commotion, and someone might even call the guards. It was very risky.

Risky? Or was it, on the contrary, the perfect solution? Maybe this was just the idea that Manu was looking for.

If there was a great uproar and confusion, the guards would arrest the culprits for sure. It was Manu's chance to find Bento. He was sure that nothing bad could happen if he was at Bento's side, even if they were at the bottom of a dungeon.

With this in mind, Manu took another stroll around the market square. Now it was clear what to do — carefully choose the best stalls, run very quickly and grab a slab of bacon here, a peach there, another fruit at another stall, always taking care to pull from the bottom of each pile, so that everything would go flying. Manu could also throw a few pieces of sausage to the dogs, so that they would begin to fight and add to the confusion.

The plan was quickly put into action. Manu crisscrossed through the buyers and sellers, running and pulling something from every stall, knocking over baskets and spilling bags filled with grain. People were running around everywhere. Some, who were also hungry, ducked down to compete for the scattered produce. Others tried to gather whatever they could and put it back on the tables. Some, baffled, sought to help one side or the other. People shoved and yelled.

"Get your hand out of there!"

"Drop it!"

It wasn't long before the brawl began. A woman rapped a child on the head and started throwing oranges at the crowd. An urchin came up behind her and hit her on the head with a melon.

"Here come the king's guards!" someone yelled.

That was the cry Manu had been waiting for. Now it was only a matter of staying in the middle of it all, so as to be picked up immediately when the guards arrived. They would grab him for sure, and in an instant he would be with Bento. To attract more attention, Manu grabbed a sausage and began to eat it ostentatiously, walking slowly through the chaos.

On one side of the plaza was a stately mansion with four steps leading to a stone porch. It looked like a small stage, all set for a performance. Well, it was time to put on a show. Manu climbed the steps of the mansion and leaned against the wall beside the heavy wooden door, nibbling from a pear in one hand and half a sausage in the other. He watched the uproar with a racing heart, feigning a disdainful smile while trembling inside.

The guards came running down a side street. They were pushing people, grabbing their arms, dispensing blows. The shouting got louder. Amid the tumult, a bearded man — tall, strong and well dressed — spoke to the soldiers with vigorous gestures, as if he were giving orders. It was impossible to pick up a single word he said, there was so much noise in the square. But from his imposing manner, he could only be their boss.

Suddenly, the man saw Manu. The child stared at him boldly. Why? The man was furious. He strode toward Manu.

Everything was going according to plan. In a few moments, Manu would be arrested and would find Bento.

All at once, the big man sprang up the steps to the house, two at a time, and grabbed the little body by the shoulders, pulling the child firmly to his side.

But then he did something unexpected.

The man wrapped Manu in his cloak and threw the weight of them both against the heavy wooden door of the mansion. With a creaking sound, it opened. Quickly, the man closed it again and secured the latch — a solid iron clasp.

Manu was trapped all right, as planned, not in Bento's dungeon but in a strange place, in the hands of an unknown, bad-tempered man.

No wonder his legs were trembling and his heart was beating so hard it seemed it would burst.

4

Don Diogo

IN THE FIRST moments of being locked inside those walls and held fast by that hefty man, Manu made a superhuman effort not to cry.

It was impossible not to be afraid, but it was necessary to hold on, whatever happened. This wasn't part of the plan, but he must not lose control. Manu needed to stay calm in order to understand what was going on and find a way out.

The man, however, did not seem willing to wait. He gave Manu a close, firm look and then started dragging him again, through entrance halls, corridors and rooms, to the back of the house. They finally reached a huge kitchen where the aroma of bread baking in the oven was so strong and delicious that it was impossible to think of anything else.

Manu heard the man ask, "Where is the madam?"

"Upstairs, sir," was the answer.

"Go get her," he ordered.

The cook's helper, who was washing vegetables in a basin, immediately stopped what she was doing, wiped her hands on her apron and disappeared.

The man gave new orders.

"Give this child a cup of milk. And see what there is for the poor boy to eat. He can barely stand straight."

Then, examining Manu from the front, he said, "He looks like a frightened squirrel."

"Scared but hungry," said the cook, as Manu swallowed the milk in huge gulps, emptying the tin cup with astonishing rapidity.

"Give him all the food he wants," the man said, in that same tone of one who was accustomed to giving orders and being obeyed. "I'll go get the madam. It's taking too long."

"Yes, sir."

The woman refilled the mug of milk. And while Manu watched, scared and not understanding what was happening, the cook talked in a continuous mumble. She complained about constantly having her work interrupted. She noted that Don Diogo was always bringing dirty, hungry creatures into the house. She said he never knew what to do with them and was always looking for orphanages, convents or homes that would welcome them. Then she announced that she was going to get ready.

"I think I'd better just put some more water on to boil. Because he's certain to ask me to fill a tub for your bath."

A bath? No! Manu did not want to take a bath, could not take a bath, would not let that happen.

He took another sip of milk and grumbled, "I'm not going to take any bath."

"Well, we'll see about that. What are you thinking? It's just arrive on the doorstep, come in, eat and bring dirt into the house? Yes, you're going to have a bath. I'm going to scrub off that crust of filth. Wash your hair. See if you have lice. And then …"

"I will not take any bath."

But seeing that the woman was really determined, Manu stopped eating. It was best to go, even if it meant having to leave the warm, inviting kitchen. He was just rushing out the door when the big man returned. They bumped into each other.

"Where do you think you're going?"

"Home. You can't keep me here against my will. I'll tell my mother."

The answer was brave and smart. But it mustn't have been very convincing.

Don Diogo replied in the tone of one who didn't believe a thing the child said, "Ah, you're going home? So you have a home? And your mother? Where is she? I'll take you there myself, this instant. That way you won't run the risk of being arrested by the soldiers who are out there abusing everyone. I want to see your home … I want to see this mother. What's her name?"

A lump formed in Manu's throat.

"And what is your name?"

Silence.

"Come on, tell me."

"Manu."

"And where do you live, anyway?"

But remembering home and their mother was too much. The lump in Manu's throat got bigger and bigger, and he couldn't form a single word.

"Leave the child alone, husband. Don't you see he's exhausted? And very scared, as you said."

The voice was soft, the tone of one who cared about the anguish Manu was going through. He looked in the direction of the person who spoke and only then saw the fine lady behind the immense figure of Don Diogo filling up the doorway. She was short and slim, with a fragile air. She had delicate features in a pale, sad-looking face.

She approached the child. "Did they give you something to eat?"

"Yes, they did, ma'am."

"There's still something more here," said the cook, putting another dish on the table. "Sit down and finish eating. Quickly, so we can get you into the bath."

There were a few pieces of stewed chicken, some onions and some boiled vegetables. It smelled wonderful, deliciously appetizing. And it was warm, just out of a simmering pot.

Manu sat down.

"Eat quickly, the bath can't wait," continued the cook, teasingly.

Then, turning to the lady, she explained, "The kid was hungry — no doubt about that. But he stopped eating and broke into a run when I told him he'd have to take a bath. We know these little piggies — they're all scared. But he won't escape me, even if I have to go get him out there amid the other piglets in the pigsty."

"Let him eat in peace."

"But, ma'am, I have a lot to do. I must take care of the kitchen. If I'm to give him a bath, it has to be now, so I don't get behind. The kettle is already boiling."

"Leave him alone," the woman repeated.

Manu sighed with relief.

But his relief was short-lived, because the lady added, "Prepare the tub and I'll take care of the bath."

There was no escape. Or was there? Manu could always try.

"No need. I can wash myself. I'm already pretty big."

The voice of Don Diogo ended the discussion.

"As long as you get clean, it doesn't matter who rubs you down. But someone needs to make sure all the dirt comes off and see if your ears are clean and that you get rid of that crust of mud on your feet … and everything else."

"Leave it to me," the lady offered once again.

Manu ate slowly, prolonging the meal as much as possible. He had to come up with some kind of inspiration. Some way to get outside these doors and walls. Some way to get to Bento.

A bath was out of the question. What an idea! What a mania for water! Fine for a fish or a duck, but not for a kid.

5

Dona Ines

WHEN THE LADY started to lead him out of the kitchen by the shoulder, Manu's heart tightened. Nobody had touched him with affection since Bento had been arrested. And her touch was unexpectedly tender, much more sensitive than Bento's. It made Manu nostalgic for their mother. He remembered her smile, so like the one on the stone statue of Our Lady on the church altar. He was seeing that same smile now.

They went through a side door, reaching a room with a stone floor and stone walls. Manu looked around. There were shelves with provisions as well as casks, bottles, hanging sausages, a string of onions and another of garlic. Maybe it was a pantry or cellar. It had two benches. On one of them, there were folded clothes. In the middle of the floor was a tub full of water.

The lady sat on the other bench, with her back to the tub.

"If you don't want me to see you get into the bath, that's fine," she explained. "You get into the water and have a scrub. Then check to be sure you got all the dirt off."

It wasn't going to work. Manu took off his coat and shirt, rolled them up and put them on the floor near the bench with the clean, folded clothes. While he was taking off his socks, the lady picked up the dirty laundry.

Manu got into the tub and cowered under the water. It was not as cold as he had feared. It was clear that water from the kettle had been mixed with cold water, which someone had brought from a well — as he used to do in the tavern and the sacristy, and as Bento used to do at home. When they had a home, that is …

Thinking about Bento and the good times brought the lump back into Manu's throat.

"But what is this?"

The lady's voice interrupted Manu's thoughts.

In a sudden frightened movement, the child pulled in his wet legs and hugged his knees, head lowered, as if expecting to be caught.

"It is so beautiful! A true work of art …"

Manu looked up and, realizing what was happening, could not help crying out, "Drop it! It's mine!"

He couldn't hold back the tears, thinking, these people took me by force, made me get into a tub of water against my will and now they're going to seize my father's gift? Oh no, they'll probably take Bento's pocket knife and Mother's rosary, too — they're all in my trouser pocket. They are all I have. I won't let that happen. No.

The lady gently placed the ceramic dove on top of the folded clothes on the bench beside her. Then she began to speak.

"Calm down … I won't hurt you or take anything that is yours. My husband was right when he said you looked like a wild creature — skittish and scared. But if you're in my house, we need to get to know each other. So I'll introduce myself. Who knows, we might even begin to be friends. My name is Ines."

"I'm sorry, Dona Ines," Manu managed to say, holding back a sob.

The lady came closer to the tub, wet her hand and passed it through the child's hair. She looked at Manu, pulling back the bangs falling over his face.

"You have beautiful eyes, long eyelashes, soft features like an angel carved on the cathedral's altar. And you were carrying a work of art in your pocket."

"It's just a toy. My father made it for me."

"It was your father who made it? But then he must be an artist!"

"He was a potter, my lady. Like so many others. But he was one of the best."

Ines realized that Manu was using the past tense. She looked more carefully at the child cowering in the bath, knees hugged.

"What's your name again?" she asked.

Her husband had asked, and the child gave the same answer.

"Manu."

The lady did not beat around the bush. She asked directly, eye to eye, "Manuel or Manuela?"

If the correct answer had been Manuel, the child might have been offended. But since it was Manuela, she burst into tears. They were tears of fear, relief, sadness, longing, all mixed together. Fear of the consequences of being discovered. Relief at not having to hide and lie to the lady, who seemed gentle and affectionate. Sadness because she was ruining Bento's whole plan to protect her by pretending to be a boy and never leaving his side. Longing for her father, her mother, her whole family. At that moment she was mainly missing Bento, who was so far away, the poor boy, in some dungeon that she could neither imagine nor find.

In the midst of her crying, she was barely able to answer.

"Manuela …"

Dona Ines wasn't angry. Manu's response only confirmed what she had suspected as soon as she saw the child. Not caring that the wet little body was soaking her clothes, Dona Ines hugged and comforted Manu, patting her on the head.

"So let's get really clean, beautiful and fragrant. Then you can tell me your story."

"Please do not tell anyone," the girl managed to say.

"I promised. It's a secret. No one can know."

"Who did you make the promise to?"

"Bento, my brother."

"Where is he?"

"I'm not sure … But I need to rescue him. He and I are the only ones left. And we promised to care for each other."

"Don't worry. I won't betray your trust. I'll just tell my husband. He can help us."

Maybe it was a good idea. There certainly wasn't a better one. And Manuela had no choice. She stayed silent and didn't agree or disagree.

Dona Ines continued, "But let's deal with that later. Now it's bath time. Scrub yourself well and then put on these clothes here." She smiled and added, "They're boy's clothes, so they won't betray your secret."

6

Don Gaspar

Lying between the sheets in her soft, new bed, her head resting on a pillow, Manu could hear various noises coming through the darkness. Outside, the street was waking up, too.

A horseman had just passed by, the *cloque cloque* of the horse's hooves hitting the cobblestones with the jingling sound of a harness and its delicate silver bell. In the distance, a rooster was singing and a dog barked. Then the wheels of a cart drummed rhythmically on the uneven roadway, indicating the arrival of sellers with their goods, ready to set up stalls in the square — the racket and momentum of a market day was about to begin. The bells of a nearby church chimed. Answering their call to mass, neighbors opened and closed doors that creaked and slammed. They were soon hurrying to the house of God.

In a few short days, Manu had learned to distinguish the first sounds of the morning. Once again she felt like going to pray herself. She wanted to ask for good fortune for her brother and give thanks for being sheltered in this home. Perhaps the church nearby also had an Our Lady with a loving smile to remind her of her mother. Like the smile she saw on the face of Dona Ines. Manu knew that they would all go to church together on Sunday. But she didn't need to be in a chapel or in front of an altar to say her prayers or talk to her parents. Over the past few days she had been doing this every night and every morning, snuggled between real sheets in her soft, warm bed. It wasn't even necessary to say a word out loud.

Mother, how lucky that the lady came to my aid just in time. I couldn't have taken any more. I didn't know what to do on my own. But Bento needs help now. Father, I know that he's older and should be able to take care of himself and that you told him to take care of me. But he didn't neglect me — what happened was not his fault. It was those guards. I saw everything from the landing, hidden behind the chest. I'm fine, as you can see. Don Diogo and Dona Ines are taking care of me. I know that my prayers were heard, that you asked God and Our Lady to bring this kind couple into my life. Thank you. Now I'm fine. But we have to save Bento. Help us, God.

Birds were singing outside, a sign that the day was really beginning. Soon a ray of sunlight would enter through the tiny window, making the dust dance in the air, bright as the stars of the Milky Way in the speckled night sky. Could the sky where her father and mother and brothers were be the same? Was there night and day there, too? Did they have the sun, moon and stars?

At night, when she thought about these things, Manu would become dreamy and end up falling asleep. But early in the morning these thoughts and memories would take wing, waking her up. Then they would quickly be interrupted by the sounds outside and the thoughts of what would happen that day.

So much had happened in the past few days in the big stone house that Manu could barely remember it all. At the end of that first bath, she put on the clothes that were on the bench. Good clothes made of fine fabric. Where did they come from?

"They belonged to my son," explained Dona Ines. "He was about your age when he died."

She wiped away a tear with one end of the towel. Manu did the same with the other end. They talked about the people in their lives who had died. The girl discovered that the plague had also marched through Lisbon, paying no heed to big city or small, old or young, man or woman. It left behind a trail of death and fear. The bishop held masses for everyone to pray for the dead and ask that the epidemic never return. The procession she and Bento had seen when they arrived in Lisbon was just one of many held for this purpose. Manu started to pray again.

My mother, as you are now close to God, talk with the mother of the child Jesus and ask her to explain to him that the plague is a very bad thing and should never appear anywhere again.

Even Don Diogo hid the tears filling his eyes when Dona Ines brought Manu to him, fresh out of the bath, her hair cut, and dressed in his son's clothes. The woman quickly told her husband the story she had just heard about the girl and her brother's adventures — their escape from the plague, her disguise as a boy, their work at the tavern, the fight, the prison, Manu's days roaming the streets.

At the end of the story, the gentleman said, "Give me your brother's full name. I will try to discover his whereabouts. Most likely he is imprisoned in the castle. I have friends who can find out."

"Talk to Gaspar," suggested Dona Ines. "You can tell him everything. My brother knows what it means to want the best for a sister."

"That's what I'll do."

Manu soon learned that Don Gaspar was a rich and powerful man who owned merchant ships that carried goods all over the world. He had connections with important people.

They had news the next day. Don Diogo arrived home to say that his brother-in-law had managed to locate

Bento, but that so far there was no chance of seeing him. There was even less chance of having him released or guaranteeing him a fair trial.

"The situation is worrying. The charges are serious. Your brother is imprisoned not just for being rowdy. He is also accused of not respecting the authorities and insulting His Majesty. According to what Don Gaspar could find out, there is no chance of him being released soon."

Manu's heart sank. She couldn't let Bento pass the rest of his days locked in a dungeon. Especially since he hadn't done anything wrong. But what could a slight young girl do on her own?

You are not alone, my daughter. You have good friends and protectors in Dona Ines and Don Diogo. Thank God for this, and see that you do not lose faith or hope.

The thought was like a reminder of her parents, part of the prayers that Manu was always saying these days.

"What can I do to help?" she asked.

"At the moment, nothing," said Don Diogo. "Even I don't know what to do. But Gaspar is helping us and will be here tomorrow night. We'll all think about what might be possible —"

"There must be something we can do," interrupted Dona Ines. "The heavens cannot tolerate this situation. The Holy Virgin wouldn't permit an injustice such as this."

The Holy Virgin has already allowed so many injustices, thought Don Diogo. Every day people saw how the heavens seemed to be totally indifferent to their pain and suffering. But he said nothing. He knew that saying something could be dangerous. The Inquisition still had eyes and ears everywhere, even though it was no longer at the height of its power. The consequences could be dire. It was important not to speak without thinking. All this just made him even more convinced that, as far as he could tell, the heavens went along with absurd and cruel things. Even with the Inquisition, it seemed.

Without saying what was going through his mind, Don Diogo came up with a few words.

"If there is any possibility of doing something, the Blessed Virgin will surely enlighten us."

Manu prayed for this revelation.

Heavenly Mother, please help us. Cast a light on our ideas. We have to think of something that will work. We must free Bento somehow. My mother, don't let my brother give up hope.

Manu spent the day making these appeals to the two mothers she prayed to. By the time Don Gaspar arrived, she was anxious, wringing her hands. She found Dona Ines's brother a little frightening. He was even bigger and burlier than Don Diogo, with a beard, huge hands and a heavy step. He spoke loudly. When he began to talk about her brother, Manu became even more worried.

"I have bad news." After a pause, he continued. "The boy has been sentenced to exile."

Manu did not know what exile was. But she knew very well what "bad news" and "sentenced" meant. She began to tremble.

"But then he will be released," Don Diogo said. "That's a lot better than rotting in a dungeon."

Rotting? Was there a danger that her brother would rot?

Don Gaspar explained. "They're going to put him in a ship's hold, take him across the ocean and leave him someplace on the coast of Brazil. He will work the rest of his life in hellish heat, among all kinds of animals and poisonous insects. Settling a new land is an arduous task. He'll need to work hard."

"But the boy is innocent," Ines protested. "He didn't do anything serious. He just got into a fight …"

"Don't give me that look, Ines. I wasn't the one who judged or condemned him," her brother said.

"And you don't have to commit a serious crime to get the penalty of exile," Don Diogo reminded them. "The law demands that punishment for lots of people — for vagrants who commit crimes like stealing bags along the riverside, for anyone who takes out their sword in a procession or sacred place, for any forger, liar or slanderer …"

"Bento did nothing!" insisted Manu.

"… or any stray, ruffian or scoundrel," completed

Don Diogo. "He was arrested as a troublemaker."

"There is nothing you can do," Don Gaspar confirmed.

The two men began to talk about crimes and their punishments, the difficulties of getting labor in the colonies, exports, sugar mills, slave labor, the African slave trade, brazilwood factories — a lot of different things that the girl could not keep up with. Then they talked about the king, who lived in Spain but who ran Portugal through his representatives in Lisbon, the wars between the Dutch and the Spaniards, and how it was necessary to restore a Portuguese king to the throne.

Manu just wanted to know more about Bento. When would he embark — and exactly where? People said that Brazil was a huge country. How would she be able to find him there? But the men talked and talked, poured themselves some wine and talked some more, and she did not know how to bring them back to the only thing that mattered — Bento's fate.

Dona Ines must have been feeling the same, because she suddenly interrupted the conversation between her brother and her husband.

"And when is his sentence being carried out?"

Don Gaspar took a few seconds to realize that she was referring to the prisoner. He said he did not know.

His sister asked another question. "And when is your next trip to Brazil? Don't you have a ship about to sail there? Can't you take him with you?"

"Maybe — that's something that hadn't occurred to me. I haven't yet set the date. It depends on receiving a shipment of goods from Seville. But maybe I can talk to a friend and offer to take the convict in exchange for his work on board during the voyage. We are no longer forced to carry exiles, but the authorities like it when we do."

The glimmer of a small hope, an idea. Thank you, Mother. Give me courage, Father. I need it because I'm going to interrupt these big men and speak directly to Don Gaspar.

"And if you manage that, couldn't I be exiled along with him? I don't mind working in the hellish heat among beasts and poisonous insects. Since he is my brother ..."

"Things don't work that way, girl. You can't travel with men on a ship."

The negative tone was firm. But the merchant's gaze was softening. He was amazed by Manu's courage and vivacity, and above all, recognized her love for Bento.

"Why not? asked Dona Ines, embracing the idea. "You only know she is a girl because we told you. She's been passing as a boy for some time, wearing men's clothes, with her hair cut. You could take her on as a cabin boy."

"Impossible. She'd have to sleep in the hold with all the sailors."

He looked at Manu again, fondly. Then he had an idea.

"But who knows? Perhaps she could be my page. Some captains use a valet. I never thought about doing that, but I could pretend to have one for this trip. And then no one would think it strange if she slept on the floor outside my cabin — they'd just think I wanted to be able to give her orders anytime. She'd always be close to me, so I could look out for her more easily."

Then he said to Dona Ines, "I can't promise, but I'll think about it. I'm doing this for you, sister. These two siblings take care of each other the same way we do. And I know that you would make sacrifices for me if need be. The way I would for you."

Hearing this, Manu looked up through the window to the blue sky outside. A beautiful day, a few clouds. Perhaps it was a good omen. She reached into her pocket and squeezed the ceramic dove that her father had given her. It was almost as if she were praying and asking the Holy Spirit, from on high, to look out for her and Bento.

7

Odjidi

MONTHS earlier, a long way from Lisbon, much farther south and on another continent, it was also a sunny day. A boy Manu's age was looking upward. He wasn't praying, though. He was just trying to figure out the direction of the wind.

White clouds were moving across the blue sky and gliding softly toward the grove of trees where Odjidi was hiding with his father, uncles, cousins and other men of the village. He didn't need to wet a fingertip with his tongue and then lift it to feel where the breeze was coming from. It was enough just to look up at the clouds. It was a light breeze, barely stirring the leaves of the trees. But the grass leaned slightly toward the hidden hunters, a sign that they were not against the wind. If they were very careful, maybe the herd of gazelles grazing below, between the trees and the waterhole, wouldn't sense their presence just yet. Maybe the animals wouldn't run off right away, allowing the men to get a little closer.

His heart pounding, Odjidi watched his father, who was crouched down, tiptoeing in front of the group. His precise gestures demonstrated his experience and confidence. The boy was proud of him. He knew that Guezo was a great hunter, admired by everyone in the village. And he was very happy because now he was grown up enough to go hunting with the men.

Odjidi knew and loved every bit of the savanna he moved around in, but he had only recently reached the age where he was admitted into the company of adults and became part of the hunting expeditions that provided everyone's food. He loved the land, its warmth, the hum of insects, the hopping of small animals. He was familiar with the roar of lions, and the hyenas' laugh that they heard at night. He was happy smelling the dry grass, or the wet earth near the waterhole where the animals came to drink. They would leave their footprints in the mud, revealing the stories of what had happened there while the men were away.

He would follow the changing of the moon and the seasons — the rains that wouldn't allow them to leave the house for days, the small fresh flowers that bloomed when the rain stopped, the green that the rains left, full of promise for harvests to come. He even liked the drought that the heat would bring, with days of warm rays beating down on the skin, and festive orange and red sunsets.

He knew the name of every tree, every bird, and every small animal that ran scared through the underbrush or quickly climbed a tree. He was learning to recognize the tracks of large animals, whose odor he was already able to make out amid the grasses.

He liked to be there, in the great silence of a thousand sounds, in the immense calm of tiny movements. It was as if time stopped and was waiting to start up again. In the savanna, he was as much at home as he was in the village.

He didn't know the forest as well. He'd only been there a few times with his father. But he knew that soon it would also be part of his territory, now that he was hunting with the men and could venture a little farther. He was getting used to that stretch of the savanna where larger trees started to appear amid the scattered baobabs and acacias and tall grass, and where he could just make out the distant green of the forest, with its rivers and fish.

It was a wetter place, with more shade and less dust, the older boys told him. The day was coming when he would hunt there. It would be yet another place where he could run free, look for food, know that he was taking part in everything. He dreamed of this day.

But now all his attention was focused on the savanna. It wasn't the time to be dreaming. He needed to follow the crouching adults. They had to get to the gazelles very slowly and silently, without being detected.

If the gazelles were frightened, there was no question of chasing them. They were too fast. But the hunters were lucky — they were skilled and the herd was large. There were always one or two animals that could be hit by a spear or an arrow, providing meat for several days.

Suddenly, with great precision, Guezo threw a spear, attacking an isolated gazelle that had strayed from the others. The other hunters' accurate strikes followed quickly, while the rest of the herd scattered on the run. The wounded animal held back, hesitant, slow, sometimes stopping. It was quickly surrounded by the group of men, who continued to attack. Their bows stretched, emptying quivers of arrows targeted at the animal they needed for food. In a few moments, the gazelle was on the ground.

Then they tied the legs of the animal and hung it on a long stick to carry it. Distracted by their work, they didn't notice that they were no longer hunters, but the hunted.

Once they realized what was happening, it was too late. Because suddenly, amid a thunderous uproar, they were attacked by a gang of heavily armed men who had surrounded them the same way they had surrounded the gazelles — silent and unnoticed.

There were many men, far more than in their group. They were strangers, from some unknown village, shouting in a strange language.

It was a tough, ferocious fight. But before long, Guezo, Odjidi and his uncles and cousins were bound more tightly than the gazelle. The attackers tied their hands behind their backs with strong ropes and put metal rings — shackles — around their necks. Each shackle was fastened by an iron chain to another man, and everyone was forced to follow in a line across the savanna until they got to the riverbank, where they were put into long canoes heading downstream.

Shortly after, when they reached the curve of the river, they were joined by others in these long canoes. More prisoners. From afar, Odjidi could see people from his village, including his mother and his two older sisters.

Guezo saw them, too. He was mad with fury. He pulled on the rope with all his strength, trying to escape and do something to free his family. It was useless. He tried again, frustrated.

"AAAAAAhhhhhhh!" He cried out like a rabid animal, a wounded lion.

The captors gave him a blow on the head. Not so hard that he fell, but hard enough not to spare him the pain. He was bleeding and dizzy and realized that it was futile to react. Desperate, Guezo looked around. He saw his son, his daughters, his wife, his brother, all his relatives and friends, caught and tied just as he was. He didn't know what to do.

They were all starting to experience very new and different things from the free life they had always lived. They had been enslaved.

8

Guezo

Lying on the hard floor that was always moving, still lashed to his companions, Guezo looked back on the past few weeks. He felt that they had all been living through a nightmare.

First they had been brutally captured. Then they were chained and transported in canoes down the river, eventually reaching the coastal lagoons. There, the attackers beat them, jerked them ashore and put them in a dark, bolted hut without a hint of light.

The place was packed. There were dozens of other men like them inside — although in most cases, Guezo could not understand the many different languages they spoke. Some of the men were from completely unknown tribes, others from hostile enemy ones.

The women and children, captured under similar conditions, were confined in another hut. One had been taken while fetching water from a creek, another when she strayed from the village to gather sticks for the fire. Some had been captured in their villages, where they were attacked when the men had gone hunting.

From the little that he managed to understand of the conversations around him, Guezo began to grasp a sense of the captors' intentions.

"That way they get used to …"

Get used to what? With that huge group of people? The darkness? The dirt? The heat? The forced immobility? Why did someone have to get used to these things?

Later, he heard some other phrases that he understood. One in particular intrigued him.

"It'll be worse on the ship, so it's good they're getting used to it now."

Ship? What ship?

Guezo had heard about groups of assailants who would show up, armed with curved swords, or arrows tipped with poisonous herbs or the venomous spines of catfish. He had heard of the danger posed by these clandestine warriors, an ever-present threat. They didn't hesitate to kill whoever fought their attempts to seize people, whether the victims were to be sold to the camel caravans crossing the desert or used to pay taxes to strong and demanding leaders in other parts of the savanna or forest. There were reports of celebrations in which the guests were seized, gagged and taken away when they were distracted and under the effects of alcohol. Guezo had heard these stories since he was a boy and repeated them to his children, warning them to be attentive and take care.

These treacherous ambushes were threats that Guezo had worried about. But his awareness of the risk hadn't stopped it from happening. They had been surprised by a well-organized attack. Now what was this new danger? What did it have to do with a ship?

Guezo had heard that the enslaved prisoners could be immediately handed over to the Jula merchants, who would take them far away to the desert or deep into the forest, never to return. Or the prisoners could be led to some market closer by, where they would be put on exhibition and offered for sale alongside other goods — piles of peppers, okra and yams, gourds of palm oil, baskets, textiles and ceramics — surrounded by goats and chickens.

A ship wasn't needed for any of that.

What were their captors going to do with them? What unknown fate awaited them?

The overheard and poorly deciphered conversations mentioned auctions, waiting to complete loading. Gradually Guezo was putting together the sparse phrases that he and others in his group were able to understand. A cousin who had traveled farther knew a language that was spoken in a neighboring village. Thanks to this, it was possible to obtain some information from other prisoners.

After a few days, they realized that they were being assembled and mixed up together on purpose, so they couldn't understand one another. That way they wouldn't try to organize themselves or create problems or plan a revolt. And they were all locked in that dark hut for two reasons.

On the one hand, they were about to make a long sea voyage in similar conditions of close quarters and darkness. It was a matter of getting used to these conditions. On the other, they had to wait there until they knew who would buy them, in what numbers and where they would be taken.

It all depended on who was willing to offer the best prices and terms on seeing the slaves. They would be exchanged for gold, weighed carefully on small scales, or for precious goods such as coral, cowrie shells, metal artifacts or fabrics like flax or wool.

When the day came, it happened exactly that way. They were sold to merchants and shipped by force — they had no idea where.

Now they were on the ship, in a horrendous cargo hold. There was the same darkness that they'd experienced in the hut, the same crowding of people, one on top of the other, with no room to move.

Only it was worse than being in the hut. Instead of being on land they were on the sea — something that Guezo had never seen before — an amazing amount of water, noisy and moving, with a strong smell. There was absolutely no hope of escaping, of jumping over the wooden guardrail and running away.

Everything was rocking constantly, at the mercy of the waves. Even the floor moved back and forth. People often felt sick to their stomachs, and many vomited. An unbearable stench of excrement combined with urine, vomit, blood and sweat permeated the hold. The only food, an awful-tasting mush, was just enough to keep them alive and prevent them from getting too thin, which would devalue the merchandise. Because that was what they had become — human goods to be sold.

To avoid the risk of becoming unmarketable, the slaves were sometimes taken, still chained, to get some exercise on deck. The exercise was necessary so their bodies would not waste away. From time to time, the slaves were even forced to dance to keep their muscles firm. Sometimes a sailor would play a flute, and someone would pound on the boards of the deck like a drum. The slaves would move to the sound of the improvised music, all but drowned out by the noise of the chains. In these moments, in the light of the sun, Guezo would try to spot a relative or acquaintance in the group.

And always, for any reason, the whip would crack to make them all obey.

Guezo tried not to think about what awaited them. But he couldn't just be a prisoner of his memory, thinking back to the independent life they'd led in the village, on the grasslands, where the animals continued to run free — the way he and his family had in the past.

He knew that his family had boarded the same ship. He had seen Odjidi from a distance, on the same side of the hold as he was. He hadn't seen his wife and daughters. Someone said that the women and children were at the other end of that dark storeroom. A cousin assured him that they had all been bought by the same dealer, in exchange for who knew how many bags of sugar and how many cowrie shells.

Guezo didn't want to think, or to remember.

He had done another dance before getting on the ship, circling the tree of forgetfulness nine times. Many of those who left — people from different tribes — did this before boarding. The captors allowed anyone to take part in this farewell dance. He wanted to, and found it good to be able to move his body. More than that, it was a way to look around, to see who else he could find and try to understand it all. He didn't dance to forget. However, maybe it would be good to stop reliving the memory of his past life.

But he knew it wouldn't change anything. He would never forget who he was or where he came from.

Nor would he ever forget this terrible journey.

9

Crossed Paths

Manu actually enjoyed the voyage. It was true that she worked hard. She helped in the kitchen and served as a page for Don Gaspar. And she was constantly doing errands, helping sweep the deck and carrying things.

She continued to pretend she was a boy, dressing in boys' clothing, as they had agreed. But now, at least, she saw Bento every day, even though they could rarely talk alone. She had given him back the pocket knife he had got from his father, which she had kept for so long. She carried her mother's rosary in her trouser pocket, and in her jacket, readily at hand, she could stroke the ceramic dove her father had given her. She thought that these were all signs that things were getting better.

In any event, she was more at ease. She was sure that soon, when they reached the village of Amparo, Brazil, she and her brother would live in freedom. Apparently, Brazil was much warmer than Portugal, which she could tell because the air became warmer each day they got farther from Lisbon. It was enjoyable even at night, when a mild breeze blew under a sky studded with more and more shining stars, a sky that was beginning to reveal stars different from those she was used to seeing with her parents at home — when she and her brother had parents and a home.

After many weeks of everything being the same, more than forty days of living between the sky and the sea, between the clouds and the waves, someone suddenly shouted, "Signs of land!"

Manu looked at the horizon and saw nothing. But someone pointed to the surface of the water.

"Look! It's sargasso."

Sargasso was a kind of seaweed that didn't exist in the high seas, she learned. Later, there were other seaweeds, including one that the sailors called donkey's tail — a tangle of herbs that clung to the rocks of the coast, lapped by the tides.

By the time night fell, Manu still had not seen land. But the next morning, she woke very early with the noisy honking of birds flying between the masts and sails.

"They're petrels," Don Gaspar explained. "These seabirds don't fly far from the coast. We're almost there."

A few hours later, she heard, "Land ahoy!"

Manu could hardly believe that this whole adventure would soon come to an end.

It was not just a matter of completing the voyage. It was much more than that. She and Bento were closing a door on a period of danger and suffering. She felt happy and full of hope. They were going to start a new life in a new land. She gave thanks to God.

All those on board rushed to the guardrail. At first they saw nothing. Only the sailor in the crow's nest at the top of the mast had seen land. But after a few hours, they began to make it out. First they saw just a line, then a range of dark-bluish hills. A little later, everything turned into a dense green vastness formed by the treetops, which from far away looked like soft velvet.

It was already getting dark when they arrived. They would have to wait until the next day to disembark. They brought in the sails, dropped anchor and went to bed, lulled by the creaking of the rigging and the *plop-plop* of ripples on the ship's hull. Manu had an unsettled sleep, full of confused dreams.

At early dawn, when all on board were preparing to lower the boats and start landing, Don Gaspar called Bento aside. He asked Manu to come as well.

"After I say goodbye, I want to be able to take good news about you both back to my sister," he said. "I don't just want to say that I left you safe and sound, as she asked me to do. I want to assure Dona Ines that I gave you good counsel and left you in good hands. I suggest that you use your judgment and don't get into trouble. When we disembark, I am going to turn you over to some priests who will be waiting on the beach. They are Jesuits. They give us letters to be taken to their superiors in Portugal and we bring them back their correspondence. I will give them the money that my brother-in-law entrusted to me for your initial expenses in this new land. And I will explain to them that you are orphans and siblings in need of protection. They will know what to do."

"I know exactly what I'll do as soon as we get off this ship," Manu said, almost skipping. "I'll stop pretending that I'm a page and barely know Bento. I'll jump onto his lap and give him a hug and lots of kisses …"

Her brother smiled.

"Yes, and I'll throw away that boy's cap and muss my little sister's hair. We'll celebrate — sing, dance and have a party — and give thanks to Our Lady of Amparo and to Captain Don Gaspar. Let's go!"

"No, none of that," advised Don Gaspar. "Best to be very discreet at first. You mustn't reveal Manu's true identity. You can do that after a few days, once the ship is loaded and on its way back to Portugal. The crew is very superstitious. Sailors often think that a woman on board brings bad luck. If they find out they were at sea in the company of a woman for the best part of two months, they may feel that they've been deceived and get angry. I might have problems on the return trip."

"If that's the way it is, don't worry," said Bento. "We'll keep it a secret."

Manu was sorry. She would have liked to have embraced the captain and given him a kiss of gratitude for helping them and reuniting her with her brother. But if she had to continue to behave like a boy, she couldn't be soft. She stood firm, thought of her father and said, almost solemnly, "Thank you, Don Gaspar. God protect you on your journey home and always. We don't have words enough to thank you."

A little while later, a small boat took them to shore in the company of the captain and some of the other sailors. And as Don Gaspar predicted, there was a priest in the midst of the small crowd that awaited them on the beach. The people were so different and so interesting that the girl barely paid attention to the information the captain gave the Jesuit about the two orphaned brothers, or the guarantees that the priest gave him to take care of them.

So this was Brazil!

Manu was fascinated by all the movement, especially by a huge red, blue and yellow macaw that was beating its wings and making a tremendous din. It rested on the arm of a man who was offering it to the sailors in exchange for some sort of tool. Just ahead, a lively and clever-looking little monkey perched on a boy's shoulder seemed to be making faces at her as it eyed her intently.

The scene was noisy and colorful. Even the people seemed to be different colors. Not just appeared to be, but were! The whites were sunburned, much pinker than they were in Portugal. And there were people with skin of all shades of brown, from reddish-colored, with straight hair, to very dark — almost black — with corkscrew-like hair, full of tiny curls. Some bodies were almost naked and were painted and covered with ornaments made of feathers. It was very different from Lisbon.

And the ways they carried things! There were baskets of all kinds, shapes and weaves, many with different geometric designs. There were boxes big and small, chests and stuffed cloth bags. Bundles. Bunches of bananas, huge watermelons. Rolls and rolls of straw mats. Large ceramic pots filled with water, carefully balanced on people's heads and so full that they were dripping along the way.

The noises also attracted the girl's attention. There were seagulls squawking overhead, whistles and chirps of birds in cages, parrots of all types and colors — they were right to call Brazil the land of parrots. Everywhere vendors screamed and yelled. There was a chaotic and cheerful din, with everyone talking at once, often in languages that Manu was sure she had never heard before. And even when the words were in Portuguese, they were spoken in a different way — more slowly, more openly. Everything was strange, but it was an attractive and festive strangeness that made you want to join the celebration.

And the smells! The sea air was similar to that on the pier in Lisbon and, in a way, was the same smell that had accompanied them throughout the journey. But now it was accentuated with the smell of huge piles of fish, both salted and fresh. The remains of fruit on the ground were rotting in the heat. And, yes, it was very hot and very humid. Everyone was sweating in the sun, even though it was morning. It seemed as if the very air was laden with sweat. It improved a bit in the shade when a breeze was rustling the leaves, which she saw were different from those she knew, with a green as intense as she had ever seen.

The fruits, too, were very different from those she was used to, except for lemons, oranges and a few others. She soon learned the names of cashews, guavas, pineapples, bananas and star fruit. But at the beginning, everything was new, and she was enjoying the novelty of this land.

Manu was also surprised by the earth itself. It wasn't just that the color was different — reddish, and distinct from the soil in their village or the clay her father worked with at the pottery. It seemed to move and have a life of its own. From time to time, the girl would shudder and lose her balance, as if the ground were swaying with the waves.

"That's the way it is," Don Gaspar explained, laughing, when he realized that the startled girl was trying not to fall over. "In the first few hours after you step ashore, you have the impression that you're still on the moving ship, and you try to right your body to fix it. But it soon passes. Tomorrow or the next day that feeling will disappear. Everyone goes through this after a long journey at sea."

The explanation was part of the captain's final farewell. In a moment, he was turning away to meet the merchants for whom he was bringing goods and from whom he would pick up a load of sugar to take back to Lisbon.

Manu was alone with Bento and the priest, who had introduced himself as Father Braz. The siblings each had their bundle of clothes.

The priest stored the correspondence he'd received in a duffel bag strapped across his chest, then picked up a basket with the various orders for goods that the captain had brought. He noticed Bento's curiosity.

"This basket is different, isn't it?" he said. "It was made by the Indians. They are very skilled and make a huge variety of woven baskets from the fibers and lianas that grow here." Then, making his way around a large building, he added, "Don't be afraid if you hear stories about wild heathens who are cannibals. Many are true, but you needn't fear because the Indians you will find here are gentle and peaceful. Only in the interior, where the wild animals are, do you find the more aggressive ones. You won't see them here in the village, in the school or in the mill."

Lianas? Heathens? Cannibals? Indians? Wild animals? Interior? Mill?

Manu had no time to digest all this information, full of words that she didn't know the exact meaning of. The three had just arrived at a large courtyard, or plaza. A very busy space came into view, opening onto a large covered arcade, with a roof supported by heavy columns.

Some men with whips were walking back and forth, while others just stared, motionless and menacing. A well-dressed man in a hat carefully examined a half-naked young man, feeling his muscles, then moved on and pulled another's lips apart to see his teeth. Farther on, a paunchy man with a moustache and a big hat was tracing his fingers along the scars on a large man's face — aiming to decipher the meaning behind those tribal marks that told a story he was unable to imagine, much less understand or respect. A bald man walked around and touched a woman wearing a blouse and skirt of coarse cloth, apparently trying to assess the qualities of her body. Whites choosing black goods.

But what made Manu speechless with amazement was what she saw in the corner of the courtyard — a group of people sitting on their heels, looking scared. They were all black people, and they were in chains, waiting their turn to be sold. They were surrounded by foremen with whips.

It was all part of the slave market.

Manu grabbed her brother's arm and squeezed hard. Bento looked at her, wide-eyed, reliving the memory of his recent arrest. They were in the company of the priest, so they said nothing, but they didn't need words. The exchange of glances between them showed what they both thought.

Where are we? What kind of place is this?

And Manu mentally corrected her first impression from a few moments before. She wasn't going to like this place after all.

10

Antonio Caiubi

THE FIRST NIGHT they stayed at the Jesuit school with a few other guests. But they didn't stay in the dormitory where the boys were sleeping — inside the white building with blue trim that dominated the flat hilltop next to a small river. They were taken to a guest house nearby.

It was a long house with a straw roof, straw walls and a dirt floor. It had no windows, only a small door. It was very smoky inside, and there were no beds. Several woven fiber hammocks crisscrossed the room at different heights, and right in the middle, the darkness was broken by a small fire that provided light and warmth, and also served to ward off insects. Some boys and young men were staying there, and before they went to sleep, they talked in a strange language.

Father Braz explained that Manu and Bento would stay there for a few days while they looked for work for Bento. The boy was willing to do any job. He had experience serving tables and helping in the kitchen at the inn in Lisbon, but there were no inns here. On the ship, Bento had done everything there was to do, even handling the toughest cleaning jobs. And before that, he told the priest, he had been a carpenter's apprentice at a cabinetmaker's workshop back in his village — at a time that was now so far away that it seemed to have been another life. He could work with wood or learn any other job.

"I guarantee you won't have trouble finding work here," said the priest. "And you'll be able to live where you work. We'll take care of that."

As for Manu, she would stay at the school. The next day, the priests would make arrangements for her to be housed with the boys under the care of Father Vicente, in the building that stretched out alongside the church. They had daily classes there in language, religion, singing, music and various crafts. They learned to read, write and do math. The school also had several workshops — for pottery, wood, metal and leather.

From the moment she heard about the pottery workshop, Manu stopped paying close attention to what the priest was saying. She remembered her father at work. She reached into her pocket where she kept the ceramic dove and squeezed her treasure tightly. She silently prayed to the Holy Spirit and Our Lady to take care of her and Bento in this new land. Would there be a potter's wheel in this place? A kiln? She wanted to feel the clay between her fingers, ready to be shaped. It would be a sign that not everything good had been lost with the changes in her life.

The next day she followed the boys when they arose early and went to church, where they all sang in a choir during mass. She couldn't participate since she didn't yet know the songs, so she took the opportunity to inspect her surroundings.

It was a very small church, little more than a chapel with a bell tower. It was the simplest Manu had ever seen — just a long hall with bare walls, a plain altar, a large door at the front and a small one at the side. The small door opened onto a garden courtyard leading to the refectory, a few other rooms, the dormitory and the priests' cells, all arranged around a cloister. But this she would find out later, when she went there with the others. Now, she saw only the simplicity of the church, with its thick whitewashed walls. She prayed a little distractedly, thanking God that she and Bento were there together, safe and sound, and asking for the divine protection to continue.

Then she began to notice the people. The day before, she had met the other three priests, all very thin, their skin burned by the sun. Now she could observe the boys. They were dressed very simply in wide-legged pants and loose shirts made of coarse cloth. All of them were dark-skinned and dark-eyed. They had straight hair, cut very short. One of them couldn't take his eyes off her.

She recognized him. He'd been looking at her ever since she arrived yesterday. His name was Caiubi, but he had been christened Antonio and that was what they should call him, Father Vicente explained. Like the others, he was an Indian, an aboriginal person. He was learning Portuguese and already understood almost everything.

But the boys all spoke another language among themselves — Avanheém, the common language. It was a language that Manu soon learned, too. It was essential to understand because different indigenous groups, who all had their own languages, used it to communicate with each other. It was a language that whites had to learn. The Jesuits had prepared grammar books and dictionaries for it. And since they had arrived, African slaves were gradually mastering this way of speaking, because they, too, spoke different languages from each other and adopted Avanheém as a common tongue.

But here in the church and in the school, Manu saw no slaves. Maybe it was the only place where the horror that had struck her at the market the day before was not evident.

Two rows back, in the middle of the choir, Caiubi still had his eyes fixed on her. Antonio, she remembered. She had to think of him as Antonio. It was his Christian name.

The songs ended. As everyone sat down on the long, backless benches, their eyes met and Antonio smiled at her.

The girl frowned. She didn't know why, but his smile bothered her.

After mass, they all went to the refectory. Just as well, because Manu was hungry. The table was set with food very different from what she was used to. There was no bread, but there was a cooked root that she had never seen. It was strange, but tasty, and had a funny name — cassava. And there was a kind of boring, dry little cake made with a coarse flour called tapioca. And fruit, always fruit. Even the fish soup that they'd had for dinner the night before had pieces of banana in it. Manu had eaten it heartily, with a big appetite after a day full of so many new things.

She'd had a scare at the end of the day when it was time to bathe in the river, and all the boys took off their clothes and went into the water. She made a fool of herself by plunging in with her shirt on, pretending to be cold and getting out immediately, abandoning the refreshing water for the heat of the evening. She had managed, but she was worried. She didn't know whether she could continue pretending she was a boy. She was sure it would be impossible to keep her secret for long.

Everything was new and different, making the time pass quickly. Early-morning classes, choir rehearsal, refectory once again. This time there was fish, and boiled corn, something she'd never had before but found delicious.

In the afternoon, workshops. Finally, it was time for pottery.

From the moment she entered, Manu saw that it was a very simple workshop — little more than a kiln and a pile of clay. They made simple bricks and tiles, with no press or glazing of the clay. There were none of the painted, colored tiles her father used to make. The girl helped to knead the clay and put it in the molds. It was good to feel it taking shape between her fingers once again, even if she was just smoothing out the shape of a square.

From time to time, she looked around. She didn't see a potter's wheel or anything to do with the making of even the simplest containers. But they must be somewhere. She had already seen a variety of pottery vases, pitchers, mugs, trays and bowls on the refectory table. Some of them even had funny names that she'd never heard before, such as moringa and cumbuca. They must be made somewhere in there, and she would be sure to find out where.

During a break in her work, while some of the boys were taking filled molds to the kiln and Manu was waiting for a new mold, the girl's fingers absently began to play with the leftover clay on the rustic table. The form of a bird started to take shape. Maybe one day she could make a companion for the ceramic dove that had traveled so far.

Suddenly, she realized that Antonio Caiubi was beside her, smiling. She couldn't be rude, so she smiled awkwardly. He made an unexpected gesture — he reached out and touched her face with the back of his hand. Then he said something she did not understand.

"Not a curumim, no."

Curumim was another word from one of those strange languages that they spoke here. But she had heard it many times in a few hours. She deduced that it referred to all of them there, the boys at the Jesuit school. But she did not understand what the Indian boy meant when he repeated it, adding something.

"Not curumim, no. Cunhã!"

"What are you saying?"

"You're not a curumim. You're a cunhã. You shouldn't be here. You should tell the priests."

Manu was startled. She realized that curumim must mean boy and cunhã, girl. It could only be that. Her secret had been discovered. Caiubi was right — Antonio, that is. Soon everyone would know. And the priests needed to know from her — they must not feel fooled. She could not begin a new life lying to the people who were helping her and who had welcomed them so generously, no questions asked. But Don Gaspar had asked …

"I made a promise," she said to Antonio. "I have to keep it secret."

"Tell one of the priests. They'll help. They know how to keep secrets."

Again, she realized that Antonio was right. She looked down shyly, uneasy at being caught in a lie when she wasn't a liar. She wanted to tell the Indian boy everything, so he wouldn't judge her badly. At the same time, she realized that she would be relieved if she didn't have to pretend anymore. Manu was grateful to the curumim for pointing a way out of the situation.

She raised her head and looked at her new friend.

"You are right. Thanks for your good advice. I'll do something about it right now."

She saw that Father Vicente was busy, surrounded by a group of boys to whom he was explaining something. She didn't want to interrupt. She went in search of Father Braz.

She found him next to the kitchen, carrying a bag of beans to the pantry. She called him aside, asked to have a private word with him and told him her whole story. She told it all at once, in a jumble, without stopping to breathe or choose words. It was like suddenly overturning a sack of grain and pouring everything to the ground at once — everything that she had kept inside. She explained that Don Gaspar had asked them not to reveal the secret while the ship was still anchored in the cove.

"But then we can tell everyone," she said. "We don't want to lie. It was just to be safe."

The priest listened in silence to the succession of surprises. Plague, being orphaned, escape, fight, prison, hunger, the soup in the sacristy, the confusion in the market square, the protection of Don Diogo and Dona Ines, exile, the voyage. The episodes followed one after another, and he listened closely as the words of Manu relived them all.

At the end, the religious man thought for a moment and said, "You were right to tell me. We'll have to make some changes. You can't keep living with the boys, bathing in the river or sleeping in the dormitory. I'll see what I can do. But rest assured, we'll keep your secret. Nothing will be made public until the ship and Don Gaspar sail back to Lisbon."

He smiled and patted her head.

"You're a brave girl. May the Virgin protect you."

"She never ceased to protect us, Father. And now she's delivered us into your hands."

"Don't worry. Now, go back to the workshop while I talk with the other priests. We'll decide what to do."

A few hours later, he came to get her. He took her to a house in the village, where he left her in the care of a widow. He asked only that the woman welcome the girl, find her a skirt or dress to wear and not let her leave the house for a few days.

That night, Manu slept on a grass mat spread on the floor of the living room. She was dressed as a girl for the first time since she had left her village, a period of time that seemed like an eternity. And now she could be called Manuela once again.

11

————

Rosa Chica

EARLY THE NEXT morning, Father Braz went to the workshop of Quim Carapina where Bento had spent the night and was beginning to work as a carpenter's helper. He told Bento that he knew the truth, that Manuela had told him everything the day before. He explained that he would not betray their secret. But he said the girl could not continue living in the school with the boys, so she had moved to the home of Dona Catarina.

"She's a good person, don't worry. Your sister is in good hands. Dona Catarina is a childless widow who is bringing up two other girls. Now there will be three, with your sister. The other two are mixed race — half Indian and half white," the priest explained. "There are many here. The settlers come from Portugal, but there are few white women."

"Yes, I'd noticed. Almost all of them have darker skin than ours. And some are quite beautiful."

The priest was taken aback. No sooner had the boy stepped ashore and barely settled — in only his second day at the carpentry shop — and he was already noticing the women? Another one who was going to be a problem in this land of heat of all kinds. He changed the subject.

"And you, how are you? What are your first impressions?"

"I'm happy, Father, very happy. I'm enjoying it here, and I know I'll get to like it even more. I'm free as a bird. The best thing in the world is freedom. Without it life's not worth living."

Just as Bento said this, two slaves passed by the door of the workshop. One was coming from the fountain with a pot full of water balanced on a cloth on his head. The other, coming from the beach, carried a pole over his shoulders from which hung two heavy baskets filled with fish. The sight dismayed Bento, but he didn't let on.

"After spending so much time locked in a cell, seeing only the dark, damp stone walls, I think everything is a wonder," he continued. "I even liked being on the ship, with all the movement of the waves. I thank God for putting good people in our path to help us. Now I'm working to give something in return and help this land produce riches for the king. Quim Carapina asked me to make a few benches, and here I am struggling with woods that I've never seen. But I haven't seen the famous brazilwood yet."

The carpenter heard the end of the exchange as he approached.

"Brazilwood isn't used in carpentry, but in dyeing," he explained. "And today it's no longer as important as it was over a hundred years ago, when our countrymen first came here. Anyway, it wouldn't show up here. The trade has become the monopoly of the crown."

"Today the wealth is elsewhere, young man," the priest added. "White sugar is a lot more valuable now than the red brazilwood. It's sugar that fills the holds of vessels going to Portugal."

"Maybe in a few days you'll see how sugar is made," said Quim Carapina. "I may send you to Don Vasco's sugar mill. He wants to place an order and we need to take measurements. I have a lot of work and can't leave Amparo at the moment."

"But doesn't Don Vasco have his own carpenters?" the priest asked, surprised.

"Of course he does — good carpenters, at that. They make the mill wheels, the grinding equipment, the troughs and yokes, the wooden trays, the roof beams, the window frames, the wheels of bullock carts — all the working pieces, as well as the furniture. But it seems that Don Vasco wants a small wooden shrine for Dona Barbara, and he needs a craftsman capable of doing something more elegant."

And so it was that a few weeks later, Bento was sent to the sugar mill to work out the details of the order. As he walked the three leagues that separated the village from the mill, he thought about the recent changes in his life.

At this point, the two siblings were feeling quite at home in the new land. They were getting used to the heat, the food, the intensity of light in the tropics. They were even getting used to the presence of slaves every-where, doing all kinds of heavy work. The slaves were like the poorest of the poor in Lisbon — people with no choice but to live in poverty and hunger, to depend on the charity of others or on pilfering. If fortune smiled and brought them some work, it was always a heavy and exhausting load, poorly paid, ruining the body — the difficult jobs that nobody wanted to do but that everybody needed to have done. Not much different from what the two siblings had experienced and seen around them their whole lives.

But Bento and Manuela also noticed some clear differences in the colony. Although the slaves in Brazil may have had fewer material needs than the poor in Portugal, they suffered much more. They had some-where to sleep and something to eat every day, because if they were too weak and frail, their work would be less productive. But they couldn't go where they wanted, they were forcibly separated from their families, and they were subject to mistreatment by their owners. That was the biggest difference — they had owners. They could be bought and sold as if they were not people, but things — merchandise. They were brought from far away, from Africa. And they all were black.

In the widow's house, Manuela helped the other two girls, Beatriz and Felipa, with the household chores. They were close in age, one a little older than Manuela, the other slightly younger. Both were daughters of an Indian woman and Dona Catarina's late husband. Dona Catarina had no children of her own and had taken the girls into her home and brought them up.

All of them worked, and there was plenty to do. The colony was far from Portugal, and almost everything had to be done at home — salting meat and fish so that it wouldn't spoil quickly, grinding corn to make cornmeal, making cassava flour, preserving vegetables and fruits. There was always work to be done on a spinning wheel or a loom to make the household fabrics. They had to make seed oil for the lamps, ash and lard soap, brooms of brushwood sticks and palm fiber, and weave nets, and mats for sleeping.

The household slaves took care of most of the work, but not all of it. Two men tended the garden of corn, cassava, beans and squash. Two women were charged with work in the kitchen, the heavy cleaning and washing clothes in the river.

There was also a boy slightly older than Manuela who chopped wood, carried water from the fountain and helped with all the household chores. His name was Didi — at least that's what everyone called him. But when he referred to himself as Didi, he put the accent on the first syllable.

Manuela liked him immediately, with his intelligent expression and friendly smile. But they could not talk much, because of a lack of time and because of language difficulties. As the weeks passed, however, and both he and she learned more words in Avanheém, they were able to share information about their lives and see that they had some things in common. She still had Bento, but had lost her parents and two other siblings to the plague. He had arrived from Africa a little more than a year before, had been separated from his family by captivity and had not had news about any of them.

Manuela told Bento all this on the eve of his departure for the mill. She was almost in tears. The boy was surprised because she had always been brave and had never shed tears needlessly. Why did she come to the workshop asking him not to travel to Don Vasco's mill?

"But it's a short way, hardly even a trip," Quim Carapina explained, smiling. "Why are you worried? It's just a three-league walk. He'll only be gone a few days."

She could not explain why she was so upset. But ever since her brother had been released from prison and they had managed to stay together, she was afraid of losing him again. She was fearful that something would happen to them if they weren't within reach of each other. And when she understood that Didi was in a situation much worse than hers, she became distraught. She was afraid of what might happen to them in a place where everyone accepted so naturally that families could be separated forever.

She tried to respond to the carpenter.

"I'll miss my brother terribly."

Then she asked Bento, "How long will you be gone?"

"The time that is necessary," was the almost harsh answer from the boy who couldn't give in to childish pleading. "And don't talk about it anymore."

Now, walking along the road under the warming sun, Bento remembered the tone he'd used with his sister and regretted not being more caring. Manuela didn't deserve it. It was true that she had been very sensitive lately, and was irritated or cried unexpectedly for no reason. She hadn't been like that before. Maybe it was the delayed effect of everything that had happened to them, and which the girl had had to keep locked inside. Or maybe it was that she was no longer a child, that she was becoming a woman. And he really didn't understand women very well.

But he knew for certain that if it were not for Manu, he'd still be in that horrible, damp stone cell in Lisbon, or suffering a lonely exile. He had already lost hope when she rescued him and brought him here. He shouldn't have been so harsh with her.

While he was thinking about all this, he disappeared into the sugar cane, the wind rippling the field as if it were a sea of intense green. It was a sight more beautiful than he'd ever seen. Under the hot sun, step by step, he completed the journey. Reaching the top of a hill, he spotted the buildings of the mill on the floodplain below. It was just as Quim Carapina said — the large two-story house with a small windowed turret, the mill with a tiled roof and its wheel turned by oxen, the chapel, the long slave quarters and a scattered group of houses. It was a small village set in a sea of green sugar cane.

The road curved, passing by some tall trees with a stream of clear water running through them. It began as little more than a trickle percolating among the rocks, then gradually swelled. Bento followed the riverbank, descending the slope of the small hill. When he reached the flat plain at the bottom, he saw a widening of the riverbed into a sort of pool surrounded by large stones, before the water continued its course a little farther on. At the pool, a group of young slave women were washing clothes and scouring copper pots with sand in a huge wooden trough. Some of the girls were very beautiful.

The boy stopped to look at them. But in an instant they saw him and were startled. One squealed, another chuckled, and they all began to talk among themselves. As he wiped the sweat from his forehead with the back of his hand, the oldest-looking one asked him who he was and what he was doing there in Don Vasco's mill.

"My name is Bento. I've come from Amparo at the request of Quim Carapina to take measurements for a wooden shrine."

"Dona Barbara has been waiting for this for a long time," one of the women replied.

The women stopped working to talk with him briefly, grateful to have an excuse to take a little rest. Only the one who was at the far end of the pool continued what she was doing. She was the most beautiful. She was rubbing sand into the bottom of a copper pot that had been blackened by sitting for hours on the wood stove. The others were doing laundry — soaping, scrubbing, bleaching in the sun, rinsing, wringing and then spreading the huge amount of clothing on the grass. It would be loaded into basins later, still damp and heavy.

"Just yesterday Senhora Barbara complained that it seemed as if the carpenter would never come. Isn't that right, Tonia?"

"I didn't hear any complaint from anyone. You're always hearing something, Carmo."

"Stop scolding me. Everyone heard, didn't they, Rosa?"

She agreed. And so, with the talk going back and forth, Bento quickly learned all the women's names. Except for the one who was cleaning the copper pot. He had to ask.

"Ah, that is Rosa."

"But aren't you Rosa?" said the boy, who had paid attention to all the names.

"I am just Rosa. I was born and raised here. She arrived last year, straight from Africa. She could only speak her own language, but she had to learn the house-work quickly. And Senhora Barbara was convinced she had to call her Rosa — why, I don't know …"

"Because she arrived on the birthday of Senhora Barbara's sister, Senhora Rosa, who died."

"Yes, but she came along with her mother whose name is Chica, so she became Rosa Chica."

Hearing her name, the girl looked up from what she was doing and stared at Bento with a haughty, almost challenging air, as if she wanted to say something. But everything stopped there. They heard the sound of horses' hooves.

"The foreman!" cried one of the slaves.

In a second, the conversation ceased and they were all working again.

Bento watched as the rider approached. He had a straw hat, and a whip in his hand. Bento thought it best to talk to him immediately, before being questioned. He explained who he was and said he had just stopped to make sure that this was the Amarante mill.

The man ordered the carpenter to accompany him and steered his horse toward the big house.

There was no other option. The boy had to follow him immediately. But he still managed to look back and smile at Rosa Chica. This time she returned it, half-mockingly.

That look and that smile made Bento stay at Don Vasco's mill much longer than necessary. He even offered to build the shrine on the spot, something that

Quim Carapina hadn't considered. But it was a good excuse to be able to see the pretty girl who worked in the kitchen and cleaned the house, and talk to her from time to time. And they all welcomed him, especially Senhora Palmira, Senhora Barbara's mother and his countrywoman. When she heard the Portuguese boy's accent, she was delighted.

"Oh, how I miss my dear homeland!"

Senhora Palmira was constantly coming to the open shed where Bento worked to ask for news. She wanted to know things that Bento couldn't answer — about the current fashions in Europe or some new music that was being played at parties. But he could describe in detail the procession he had seen just after arriving in Lisbon, giving thanks for the end of the plague — the quilts hanging from the balconies, the chants, the branches decorating the window grills, the flickering candles carried by the faithful, who wound their way through the hills of the Bairro Alto toward the center of the city.

Senhora Palmira listened and sighed.

"Oh, how beautiful! I guess I'll never see anything like that again. Now my life is here. I came as a girl with my father, and I never returned. But it makes me very happy to hear you talk. It takes me back to Lisbon."

One time, Don Vasco heard her and joked, "It takes you back in thought but without your stomach churning with the rolling waves, isn't that so, Mother? You always say that you were nauseated the whole trip over."

"I thought I was going to die. I vomited so much my guts almost came out."

"So be happy now that the words of Bento the carpenter can take you from Amarante back to Lisbon."

Everyone laughed. And Bento continued telling them his memories of the inn, the street market, the fight he'd been in. Then he added, "I didn't have a chance to see much. I had some problems at work. But my bro ... my sister can tell you more sometime. In fact she lived with a nobleman's family for a while."

Everyone was interested, asking how it had happened. Bento enjoyed being the center of attention. He told them about life in his village, the banter of his siblings, his father's craft, his mother's work, the garden with cabbages right outside the house with the blue and yellow glazed tiles. He recalled how neighbors gathered to tread the grapes in the winepress to make wine. He remembered the olive oil, the long winter nights, the soup by the fire. He didn't talk about his arrest or his exile, although he already realized that in this new land no one cared. There were other exiles, or former prisoners. The past didn't matter. If a person worked hard and was friendly, all would be well.

On Bento's first night at the mill, the other carpenters asked him to sit with them around the campfire in front of the slaves' quarters. They were all slaves. It was his turn to listen. They had sad stories of a terrible journey in a crowded ship's hold, maltreatment, other owners, other places, family separations. They were homesick for their native lands, very different from the one he and Senhora Palmira came from.

But the conversation didn't last long. Everyone had to go to sleep early, because more work was waiting for them when the sun rose.

The next day, as he was taking a bench he had repaired back to the kitchen, Bento found Rosa Chica by herself.

Unexpectedly, she asked, "Brother or sister?"

At first, Bento didn't understand. The girl explained. She had noticed his hesitation the evening before and was wondering if, after all, he had a brother or a sister. He wanted to tell her the truth, and that's what he did. He quickly mentioned his two dead brothers, and the young sister who had fled from the plague with him, who had dressed as a boy and saved him from prison.

"I had a little brother who died when they captured us, and a sister who died on the ship," Rosa Chica said. "My mother was bought by Don Vasco along with me and works here, too. But I have another brother who I've never seen again. And I don't know what happened to my father. Some of the other women saw them on the ship, so they may not be very far away."

"No use talking about it, my daughter," Chica broke in. She was bringing in a basket of sweet potatoes to peel. "It only makes us feel bad. What can't be remedied must be endured. It can stay with you forever, like these scars we bring from our land. But since there is nothing you can do, it is best forgotten."

Rosa saw her mother's sad look. She gazed at her beloved face, with the tribal scars from the other side of the sea, and was silent. She had tears in her eyes when she looked at Bento.

The boy smiled and reaching out, gently squeezed her hand. Then he was silent.

But later they found a way to talk some more. Bento listened attentively to what Rosa Chica wanted to tell him — her memories of her father and brother, her sense of longing and her determination to find some clue about where they were. Bento wanted to help. He asked for more details, and promised he would do everything possible to try to get news of her family when he returned to Amparo. It was a bigger place. Maybe someone there knew something.

12

Queen Jinga

BENTO RETURNED from the mill full of news. At first, Quim Carapina was annoyed that the boy had stayed in Amarante for so long. But then he realized that the time had been worthwhile. For one thing, the order for the wooden shrine was settled. Not only had Bento taken measurements, but he would soon begin to make it. It had already been paid for and was now one less thing to worry about. Furthermore, the new helper's work had been highly praised by the women in the house. And Don Vasco had taken the opportunity to order another piece of furniture — a canopy bed, something that had never existed in those parts. Senhora Palmira remembered seeing one in Lisbon when she was a girl, in a noble house where she had gone with her mother, an embroiderer, to deliver some sheets. It would pay good money.

Manuela was happy that her brother was back. She had really missed him. She also had lots of her own news to tell. She was doing well at the Jesuit school, learning a lot. And, happily, she was really improving in her work at the pottery.

Better yet, in the opinion of Bento, the girl was feeling less lonely. She was good friends with Beatriz and Felipa. The three spent the day talking as they worked — an endless, soft-spoken patter, like the twittering of the sparrows that gathered in the late afternoon in the branches of the huge sibipuruna tree in the church square.

Through all her conversations with the two girls, Manuela had mastered the common language and could express herself much more easily than when she arrived. She was able to follow the lessons at school and chat with her friends. She was so talkative that Father Vicente had called her attention to it more than once. The teacher decided to take advantage of the girl's aptitude for talking and teach her how to read. Then she could read the prayer book aloud to everyone during meals or while the others worked.

It wasn't common for a girl to learn how to read. But Manuela was different and everyone accepted it. She had arrived dressed as a boy, she knew how to shape objects out of clay, she made friends with the Indian boys. Especially with Antonio Caiubi, who had won her confidence. They talked together for hours. He told her about life in the forest — the hunting, fishing, celebrations and animals. She, in turn, spoke about crossing the wide sea, the opulence of the altars in the stone churches across the ocean, the roads with carts laden with hay passing through wheat fields and vineyards, the rolling hills covered with olive trees that promised olive oil.

But now her friend was no longer in Amparo. As he had explained to her, the Jesuits brought boys from the Indian villages to stay for short periods. They would teach them for a while, then exchange them for other village boys, while the first group returned to their people. Then the first group would come back again, always taking turns. Thus they learned to pray and sing, studied the religious doctrine, developed the rudiments of a trade, but allowed others to have the opportunity as well. And that way they weren't away from their families for long.

"So you stand between the village and the town, with one foot in the hut and the other in the school," she had said, acknowledging the benefits of the system.

Manuela was missing him. She and Caiubi had become very attached to each other, especially when Bento was away. Even now, though Bento had returned from the mill, the young carpenter was very busy and hardly had time for her. Gradually, the girl became inseparable from Beatriz and Felipa. And when she missed male conversation, she began to talk a lot with Didi. Little black Didi, as they called him in the house.

In the early days, the two had spoken to each other about their suffering, their pain, their sad memories. Now they were beginning to talk about their good memories and to tell the stories that they'd heard from parents and grandparents during the happy times when their families were together. Often these stories involved strange animals.

"What is this *wolf* you mentioned?" the boy wanted to know.

"Similar to a dog."

"And a *bear*?"

"It's much bigger."

"Like an elephant?"

"I don't know. I've never seen an elephant."

"It's huge. But a bear, is it like a giraffe? Or does it have stripes, like a zebra?"

Manuela laughed. "How should I know? I don't know what giraffes look like. I've never seen this zebra you're talking about."

He took a stick and drew in the sand to show her.

She laughed again. "You can't draw. Who ever saw a long snout like that? And those big ears? And this other creature with that long, thin neck. Is it a stork? But without a beak and with four legs? It doesn't exist!"

"Yes, it does exist. It's you who don't know anything."

"So tell me their names. This one is a zebra?"

"No, a zebra looks like a horse, only it has stripes.

This one with the long neck is the giraffe."

"And the one with the big snout?"

"That's the elephant, the largest of all. Almost the size of that quitungo."

"Quitungo?"

Manuela puzzled over the word and looked to see what Didi was pointing at. It was a kind of hut on the beach, with a simple thatched roof and no walls, where the fishermen kept their nets and trays of salted fish. Another new word. Only this one had come from Africa like Didi.

At other times, they told stories of kings and queens. Manuela remembered tales her grandmother had told her of powerful kings, and knights who rescued princesses locked in castle towers. And Didi often had to retell the stories that Manuela loved to hear about Queen Jinga.

"This is not a story. It's true. And it took place not long ago," he explained.

It was better than any invented story — about a powerful woman, there in Luanda, in Africa, daughter of a king and sister of a prince, who led armies and defeated invaders.

"Queen Jinga had thousands of Jaga troops, in many quilombos."

"Quilombo? Jaga? What are they?" Manuela puzzled over the terms. She was always learning something from Didi.

"Jaga is a nation of fierce warriors. Soldiers. And quilombos are their camps, their fortresses. She commanded them all. She made alliances, started wars, negotiated peace treaties. Everybody respected Queen Jinga. And, if you didn't respect her …"

"What happened?"

"She taught respect. My father once told me that when she went to meet the governor of the Portuguese to discuss the end of the war, he sat on a throne but didn't offer her a seat."

"That certainly doesn't show respect."

"Ah, but she taught him. Wait and listen to the end of the story. Queen Jinga called a slave and made the woman kneel on all fours, like a bench. Then she sat on the slave's back and talked as equals. That taught that governor a lesson."

Courageous, thought Manuela. And very bold. But one detail in the story left the girl puzzled.

"But Queen Jinga had slaves, Didi?"

"Of course, she was a powerful queen. All powerful kingdoms enslave their enemies. My father told me that in the end, she left that slave behind. It was like saying that when you're very rich, you don't need to carry your bench from place to place, because the kingdom had many more slaves who could travel on their own two feet."

There was a lot that Manuela didn't understand. Was Didi a slave of the Portuguese in Brazil because his people were defeated by the same king that Bento had been accused of offending in the tavern fight? What if the Portuguese had been vanquished by Queen Jinga? Then Manu and her brother might have been in Africa, living the lives of slaves as Didi was in Brazil. Separated from one another, abused and sold, having to work without ever resting.

There were lots of questions rolling around in her head. But the girl said nothing. This subject was too painful to talk about with Didi, since there was nothing he could do to break free.

Her friend, however, seemed to continue to think about the story he had told. After a short silence, he said, "I think she only had slaves who were former enemies that she had won during a war. Like all kings. I don't think she captured people from far away, in the middle of the savanna, to sell to the whites' ships to make money. My father told us something else. Many slaves who were caught by traders but managed to escape would seek out her armies. They preferred to be soldiers in the quilombos of Queen Jinga, who protected them all. And even though the whites were threatening her and demanding the slaves, she never turned them over."

Could it be that the slave-bench was an enemy warrior then? Manuela wondered.

Perhaps this same idea was going through Didi's head, mingled with his memories of freedom. Or perhaps he

was missing his father, who had told him all these stories. He was silent, thoughtful. He left Manuela quietly
to go back to work.

13

Quilombo

SOMETIMES WE hear something for the first time and it seems to loosen a knot, because immediately after, the word starts coming up over and over again. That's what happened with Manuela and the word quilombo. She had never heard the word before talking to Didi. But that very afternoon, she heard it again.

Leaving the workshop for the day, Bento passed by Dona Catarina's house to see his sister. He found her with her friends at the front door. He said something funny to Beatriz and Felipa, and laughed along with them.

Hearing a male voice amid the girls' conversation, the widow came out to see who it was. She welcomed Bento with a smile, asked him inside and offered him some juice from custard apples, sweetened with brown sugar.

Suddenly, Dona Catarina asked, "Tell me something, Bento — you who have walked to Don Vasco's mill. Have you heard anyone talking about quilombos?"

"Very vaguely. They say there are some in the interior that have been there for a while now."

"That's all?"

There was a little more, Bento remembered. He clearly recalled a conversation one night around the campfire near the slaves' quarters. The flames made Rosa Chica's eyes shine as she listened in silence to the other slaves. The boy would never forget the light puff of air that passed like a breeze over the group assembled under the stars. But he felt that to talk to Dona Catarina about this would almost be a betrayal of those who had welcomed him into their confidence. He recognized that some mysterious mutual affection was beginning to connect him to Rosa. The slaves gathered there that night were his friends. He wouldn't reveal anything about the small treasure they were holding onto — the tiny spark of hope that lit up the night, riding on words that inspired fragile dreams of freedom. Not until their day had come.

"Well … yes, that's all I know. That's what was mentioned. I once overheard a group of slaves and realized that they were talking about a quilombo, but as soon as I got close they changed the subject. I don't know what they were saying."

It wasn't much. Dona Catarina looked at him as if expecting him to say something else. Bento thought he had better cover it up a little more.

"But it showed me that no one really believes that quilombos exist. They're just remnants of African legends, or stories spread by bush captains and foremen to fool simpletons. I think some foremen even encourage slaves to escape so they can trap fugitives from other mills and get new slaves without having to go to auction."

Dona Catarina had her doubts.

"What people are talking about here is just the opposite. They say that there are these camps called quilombos. They're real fortresses. They say the slaves who escape search for these camps. Apparently in the middle of the forest there are whole villages inhabited by runaways."

She paused and then continued, "But maybe they don't exist. Maybe you're right. How would these runaways be able to find their way there? And how could they survive in such hostile jungles, full of poisonous beasts?"

A slave brought in a tray with a pitcher of juice and mugs, the widow stood to serve, and the subject changed. Bento asked his sister about her work at the pottery. She showed him a small figure modeled out of leftover clay.

"You take after your father, girl," her brother said. "What a beautiful parrot! Maybe it's not quite as perfect as the ceramic dove, but you're on the right track. Do you still have the dove?"

The girl went to get her father's piece. Everyone admired it, and they continued to talk about the beautiful glazed tiles in Portugal and the difficulties of life in the colony. Then, when Bento said goodbye, Manuela walked with him to the fountain in the square.

Now that they were alone, she took the opportunity to ask, "But do those quilombos really exist, brother?"

"I think so. It seems that slaves throughout this whole region have fled there when they could."

"If I were a slave I would also find a way to escape," she said decisively.

"I don't doubt it. You've already shown what you can do. But you mustn't talk about it in front of strangers. They wouldn't understand. First, there's no need for others to know our background. And second, they might think we want to help slaves escape, and that's a crime. After all, we never know what life is going to bring us."

He lowered his voice and added, almost secretly, "It may be that one day we will be the ones to help someone. And so it wouldn't be good for anyone to distrust us."

Manuela listened to what he said in silence. She agreed with a nod.

Bento looked her in the eyes and said, "But I'm very happy to know you're still the same and that, if necessary, those who dream of freedom can count on you."

He was thinking of Rosa Chica. Manuela immediately thought of Didi.

"You're right." She paused and added, "I even have some ideas to help them cope with the jungle and the poisonous animals."

Bento looked at her, surprised.

"What ideas?"

"I still need to think about them. But I have friends …"

The girl was thinking about Antonio Caiubi, who would soon be back from his village for a new season at the Amparo Jesuit school. Lately, ideas about how to help Didi escape had been going through her mind. After her talk with him, she realized that he had been very interested in quilombos for a long time. So Manuela had brought up the matter with the Indian boy before he left and discovered that he had a good idea where the fugitives' camps were. Since then, she had begun to think that they needed to make a plan to help Didi escape. But it was all still very vague, and she didn't want to talk to anyone about it yet.

"Some of the boys are your friends? That's very good!" her brother said, interrupting her thoughts. "That helps a lot. After all, it's hard for a girl to escape alone, or only with another woman."

Manuela could not know that he was thinking about Rosa Chica and her mother.

"A girl? What are you talking about?" she asked.

"We'll talk another time," was his answer. "I also need to think about it more. But pay attention to all you hear about quilombos. And don't let on about your interest in them."

"Who are these women?" Manu insisted.

"You don't know her. It's a friend of mine, and her mother. A beautiful girl and a lady with scars on her face.

If only she had her brother around. They talk so much about this Odjidi, so dear to them … They remind me of you when I was in prison — according to what everyone said, you wouldn't talk about anything else. But go back home now."

They said goodbye and Manuela went home. Her friends called her to play with them, and she ended up not having much time to be alone with her thoughts. Only later in the evening, before bed, did something else occur to her.

But it was an idea so tenuous and fragile that she wasn't sure how to make it work.

14

A Meeting

THE NEXT FEW weeks passed without incident, following the usual routine. Work, heat, one day after another in which Bento didn't leave Amparo and Caiubi didn't return from his village.

The young carpenter was eager to return to Don Vasco's sugar mill but hadn't come up with an excuse. The canopy bed was delayed — Quim Carapina had to finish other furniture before he could devote himself to it. Bento worked on a design for the bed and, in his spare time, made a couple of wooden candlesticks for the mill's chapel. Senhora Barbara had said that she'd like to have some nice ones for the altar.

But Bento's readiness didn't change things much, because Quim really needed his help in the workshop. The need to deliver the large candlesticks was a good pretext to return to Amarante, but it wasn't enough. And when the boy insisted that he had to deliver them before the feast of St. John, which would be celebrated at the mill, the carpenter said, "Then let's ask someone else to take them."

Bento changed his mind and stopped trying to persuade Quim. He wanted to go back to Amarante himself, not send the candlesticks with someone else. So he tried to concentrate on his work.

But it was true that the pieces he'd sculpted from wood were exceptional. Everyone who entered the workshop was astonished when they saw the carved candlesticks leaning against the wall in the corner. And so it was that one day Father Braz, after offering many compliments, ended up making a proposal.

"Quim, the other day at the school we were talking after dinner. Father Olympio said that our church altar was too plain, and it would be good if we could find a way to make it more elaborate. All the priests agreed, but we weren't sure how to proceed. None of us knows how to paint or has the time to do it."

"A beautiful altar is not just a matter of paint. You could have a painting in the background, but it would be even more lovely with beautiful statues of carved wood, Father," suggested Quim. "We can think of something."

"Well, that's what occurred to me when I saw how Bento made such exquisite candlesticks. He is very skilled at woodworking. Maybe he could make an image of a saint for us."

"Or an entirely carved wooden altar, Father," said Quim. "That would be a good idea. Bento is very accomplished, and he will certainly be able to make a beautiful, well-crafted piece."

Bento overheard the discussion and became a little confused. He liked the compliments, but he was worried about not being able to manage something so difficult. He would like to try, but did not want to be held up in Amparo when his heart just wanted more and more to go to Amarante to talk to Rosa Chica.

He didn't know what to say. But since Quim didn't raise the subject with him that day, he didn't have to say anything.

Manuela was eager to exchange some ideas alone with Didi, but couldn't because Beatriz and Felipa were always with her. And because she wanted to see if she could find out anything about the quilombos, she was very careful. She remembered Bento's warning and wanted to make sure no one would suspect she was the boy's friend, and was interested in the subject of slaves escaping and seeking refuge.

One afternoon after lunch, when the sun was strong and everyone else in the house was resting, she decided to take a walk to the beach. On the way she met Didi, who was filling a barrel of water at the fountain. He would be taking it back to the kitchen in the house. It was very heavy — he had to do such difficult work, which was made even more punishing because of the heat.

As soon as he saw her, the boy motioned for her to come over.

When she got close, the girl noticed that Didi's eyes were swollen and he was holding back tears.

"What happened?" she asked.

"A little while ago … it was a terrible thing. When I went to the canoes to order fish for dinner tomorrow, as Dona Catarina asked …"

"I know, I heard her tell you."

"When I arrived, there was a bullock cart on the beach, and some slaves were unloading sacks of sugar. They were filling a boat to carry the load to the ship anchored in the cove.

"But their foreman was angry. He was screaming and threatening them with punishment — I don't know why. They were all very frightened."

Manuela imagined the scene. That kind of situation was very common. She understood perfectly how much it would disturb Didi.

He continued, "An old man couldn't handle the weight he was carrying on his back and fell. A younger slave ran to help him and took a blow from the foreman. I felt terrible. And since there was a pitcher in the quitungo, I asked the fisherman to borrow it and quickly went to the fountain to fetch some water for them. But it got worse. When I tried to give them a drink, the foreman pushed me, tipped over the pitcher and beat them some more. It was my fault …"

The girl tried to console him.

"Don't think like that, Didi. It wasn't your fault. It was just wickedness. They were already being beaten."

"Yes, it was my fault. If I hadn't got involved, they wouldn't have been beaten again."

"Don't blame yourself. You didn't do anything wrong, only what God commands — give drink to the thirsty. Wasn't that what Father Vicente was saying in mass on Sunday?"

Manuela couldn't find the words to comfort him. The boy sobbed, rubbing his eyes with the back of his hand.

"But that's not all," he added. "It's that I was really dumb."

"How?"

"It's that I recognized one of the slaves, the younger one who was defending the older man. From a distance I thought it was him, and as I got closer I was sure. I should have been smarter. Instead of making this mess, I should have found a way to quietly get close enough to talk, to find out where they're living, which mill they're at. But I was stupid, stupid, stupid! Now I've ruined everything."

He burst into tears again. Manuela waited for him to calm down. She looked around, afraid that someone would see them and wonder what was going on. She wanted to help her friend and did not know how.

Suddenly, Didi raised his head, looked at her and said, "It was my father, Manuela. He was there, right next to me. And now he's been taken away — I don't know where."

Determined, the girl promised, "Leave it to me. I'll find out."

15

Discoveries

EVERY DAY after lunch Manuela walked to the beach to try to get information. She went when the fishing boats were coming in, thinking it a good pretext for being there if the bullock cart were to arrive from the mill where Didi's father was a slave. She told everyone that she was feeling the heat and did not like taking a siesta as the others did. She said she preferred to enjoy the afternoon breeze, sitting under a tree facing the sea.

With time, she got to know all the fishermen. She made friends with some of them and was even offered a few small fish from time to time. They were delicious fried up.

One day, one of the fishermen started to tell the girl and his helper why he preferred to brave the waves than to farm the land.

"I've been on the water since I was a child. I come from a family of sailors. My grandfather and father were both men of the sea. That's how I came here. I was put on a ship as a cabin boy when I was very young."

"But you're not afraid? It's so dangerous," said the girl.

"There are dangers everywhere. I'm used to the hazards at sea. And I like to feel free, with the vastness of the world in front of me."

That was something Manuela understood.

"You've made a good choice."

She thought a bit. She watched two slaves who were digging a ditch just ahead, under the strong sun, and added, "For those who can choose … not everyone can."

The fisherman stopped gathering and folding his net to put it up to dry. He looked at her searchingly.

"You must be careful what you say and do, girl. You have a good heart, but you can't solve the world's problems. Things are as they are, and often there is nothing you can do."

"I don't know what you're talking about."

"Well, I know exactly what I'm talking about. You're always wanting to chat with that black boy who was helping the slaves on the beach here the other day."

She pretended she didn't understand.

"What black boy? What slaves?"

"That Didi, who tried to give water to the Matoso plantation slaves when they were here with the load of sugar."

"Didi is Dona Catarina's slave and works at home, so it's natural for me to talk to him. But I don't know what you're talking about, and I don't know the Matoso mill."

"Well, you should know the landowner's reputation, so you'll be careful. He's rich from a lot of sugar and a lot of slaves. He lives about five leagues west of town, near the dense forests. And his foreman is the most vicious in these parts. From what we know, he has even killed some slaves. Tell your friend Didi not to get in his way. It could be very dangerous."

The girl's heart was pounding. Was it excitement from having heard the information she wanted or fear for her friend? Not to mention the certainty that Didi's father was in a terrible situation in such a foreman's hands. Whatever it was, a shiver went through her body.

"These are dangers much worse than the sea," the fisherman said, bringing his advice to an end.

Another shiver coursed through Manu. The fisherman noticed.

"You're getting goosebumps. The south wind is strong today. Better get going before you catch a cold."

She followed his advice. She couldn't wait to tell Didi the news, as soon as they had a chance to be alone.

But when the opportunity arose, it was short-lived. The boy was bringing in wood for the stove, going in and out of the kitchen, which was full of people. Then Dona Catarina went to fetch something from the living room, and the two women slaves left for the chicken coop. Manuela took the chance to ask Didi something that suddenly seemed very urgent, because she knew that Bento would finally be taking the candlesticks to Amarante the next day.

"Why do you always say that your name is *Di*di, not Di*di*?"

"Because I am *Di*di. It's my name. It's the name my father and my mother gave me when I was born."

"Odjidi?" She said it slowly, emphasizing the accent on the second syllable.

"That's right," he confirmed. "You finally got it right."

She breathed deeply and asked another question.

"And your mother has some scars on her face?"

"Yes, she does — three short, thin lines, one beside the other on her left cheek. Why do you ask?"

They could hear Dona Catarina's footsteps in the hallway.

"It's something I've been thinking about. I'll tell you later," the girl said.

And, almost skipping toward the door, she asked Dona Catarina, "Can I go to Quim Carapina's shop? I want to say goodbye to my brother. He's leaving early tomorrow morning for Amarante."

"Of course you can, young one. And tell him that I hope he has a good trip."

And so the next day, on his journey to Amarante, Bento was carrying more than passersby might guess.

He was pulling a mule loaded down with a pair of heavy carved wooden candlesticks — this everyone could see. But he was carrying much more. Maybe it was just a hunch, an unfounded idea, the dream of a girl. He remembered Manuela's excitement when she talked to him the day before. Maybe she was right. Maybe Rosa really was Didi's — actually Odjidi's — sister. Maybe the ritual scars engraved on Chica's face so many years ago in Africa were now a kind of map, indicating a path for the exchange of family news. Maybe one day they would be reunited. Who knew what else might happen to them following these discoveries?

Bento needed to be careful not to raise false hopes in Rosa and Chica. But he knew very well that he was carrying a cargo more precious than candlesticks, however invisible and weightless it might have been. He carried a faint hope.

16

News

THE CANDLESTICKS that Bento made for the Amarante chapel were very well received and praised by all. Senhora Barbara was delighted with them and got excited thinking about other pieces and asked about the wished-for canopy bed. Don Vasco was so enthused he planned a party to take place a few months later, on the feast day of St. Gonçalo, the patron saint of the mill to whom the chapel was dedicated.

The young carpenter was received with admiration beyond the simple but heartfelt hospitality that ordinarily welcomed visitors. When everyone gathered on the porch after supper at the end of that first day, Bento was treated like a trusted family friend. He talked a lot with everyone in the household and recounted the news of Amparo.

But later he found time to take a stroll. He walked by the mill under the moonlight and went to the small fire in front of the slaves' quarters where the slaves talked just before going to bed.

There, too, he was welcomed. Everyone had noticed his special fondness for Rosa Chica and the respect with which he always addressed her mother. They also felt that the young carpenter was interested in them — their stories and their destiny. So nobody was surprised that night when he asked one of the young slaves how he had been captured.

The boy told the story of how he and two friends had been attacked late at night when they were returning from a market a long way from their village. Bento repeated the question to Chica and Rosa. They said that they had been captured with other women and children in their village by a group of armed men, and then were taken in a long canoe down the river.

"But where were the men of the village?" he wanted to know.

"They had gone hunting," Rosa explained.

"Even my Odjidi," Chica sighed. "It was the first time he went out to hunt with the men on the savanna. I never saw my dear boy again, and now he's becoming a man."

"But some people saw him," Rosa added. "A neighbor said she saw my father and Odjidi from a distance when we were in the canoe and they were brought tied up in another boat. And I know they came on the same ship as we did, because many people told us they'd seen them. But we never saw them ourselves."

The stories were confirmed. Manuela had told her brother the same story of how Didi was captured. And he and his father had also been transported in the same ship. Most of all, the names were very similar — almost identical. Didi must be Chica's son and Rosa's brother. Bento checked one more detail. He asked the name of their village. It was the same. And he learned that Chica's husband was named Guezo.

These were two new pieces of information that he would take back to Amparo, just to make sure. They would nourish the flame of hope.

For now, he wouldn't say anything to the two women. It could all be a coincidence. In fact, Bento had no idea if this was the usual way of capturing slaves in African villages, or if these names were as common as José or Maria in Portugal, or if many women's faces were decorated with the same kind of scars as Chica's when they married or had children. He knew little about those lands and those people and could not get all the information he needed. He would talk about it with Manuela and Didi. But he hoped to return to Amarante soon, bringing Rosa news of her brother.

Bento was thinking about all this as he walked back to Amparo. From a hill, he looked down on the houses of the village and the emerald waters of the little creek. He was happy. He was bringing good news and a large furniture order that would certainly oblige Quim Carapina to send him back to the mill. He gave the mule a friendly pat on the neck, saying, "I shall return often, and soon!"

When he arrived in the village, he saw Manuela running toward him. He dismounted and held the animal's halter, thinking that maybe his sister wanted to climb up and join him for the final part of the journey.

But before he could say anything, the girl hugged him and then, hanging from his neck, said in his ear, "We have great news! I'll tell you later."

Quim came along to find out how the candlesticks had been received and to make sure that the payment had been made, so the siblings' conversation was cut short. It was only at dusk that the two were able to be alone. They sat on the sand in front of the rippling tide watching the full moon rise.

"Yesterday, just after you left, someone came here from the Matoso mill," Manuela said. "They came to get salted fish and whale oil."

"Did Didi's father come?"

"No, not this time. And I don't think he'll be coming anymore."

Bento's heart sank. Had he died? Or been sold? Just now, when it was possible to tell Rosa and Chica that there was news of him?

"What happened?" he asked worriedly.

"He was punished. He was put in stocks and lashed until he was half-fainting and sick. But it wasn't as bad as it seemed. He acted sicker than he was and just pretended that he was dying."

"How do you know?"

"That's what the old man said. The old man who was carrying the load and fell down the day that Didi tried to give water to the slaves. He brought a message from Bartholomew."

"Slow down, I'm getting lost. Who's this Bartholomew?"

"It's Didi's father. The old man said that he recognized his son that day, but didn't let on. He's a smart man — he knew how to wait for the right moment. And so he pretended to be almost dying there in Matoso, after the lashing. When the guards were distracted, he escaped. It looks as if he had a plan all ready to go. He walked into the water or went downstream on a raft hidden someplace. The dogs lost his trail in the river. But before he left, he asked the old man to tell his son what had happened. He said that he was escaping to a quilombo. He didn't say which one or where it was. But he promised that they would meet. Didi believes the story and is very excited. I've been dying to tell you what happened."

It was big news, for sure. More than what Bento had to report.

"Well, I thought I had something important to tell you. I found out how Rosa and her mother were captured, and more about her brother, and it's exactly the same as what Didi told you. And I also learned the name of the village they come from. I was sure that I'd established a family connection between them. But now I'm not so sure …"

"Why?"

"You tell me his father's name is Bartholomew. But Rosa's father is named Kezo or Guezo or something like that."

"That doesn't mean anything. We need to check with Didi. Did you forget that the slaveowners give their slaves Christian names? As I recall, the old man used a surname to speak of Didi's father. I thought it was Guezo. But it could be the other one you said. Who knows?"

17

———

Caiubi's Wisdom

THE NEXT FEW days were intense. Bento and Manuela took every opportunity to talk to each other and exchange ideas with Didi.

They were soon connecting one thing with another and discovering the links in all the information they'd gathered. They were sure that Rosa and Chica were Didi's family, and he was thrilled to know where they were. Amarante was not far away. Sooner or later it would be possible to create an opportunity for them to meet. And until that day came, Bento could take and bring back news from time to time. Don Vasco was not known to mistreat his slaves like other owners, or like the foreman at the Matoso mill. Amid the horrors of captivity, at least that was a relief. For Manuela it carried a glimmer of hope.

The days turned into weeks.

Bento couldn't start making the furniture for Senhora Barbara and Don Vasco, because Quim Carapina had told the priests he would work on their job. So the boy had to start on a different carving than he intended — the church altar in Amparo. It was a difficult and delicate craft, digging out the hard wood, trying to bring to light the shapes sheltered inside the fallen trees. First he made a rough attempt that he then smoothed over and sanded, bringing out tiny details.

This work took all his time, but gave the young craftsman a great deal of satisfaction. He remembered how, since he was a child, he had liked to work on small chips of wood with the pocket knife his father had given him. It was the only object he still had that was a concrete reminder of the family and the house where he grew up, on the other side of the vast blue-green ocean. But he wasn't using it now. He had new tools, more varied and more appropriate to the size of the work he was doing.

And how he loved what he was doing. The angels were multiplying, the bunches of grapes and the interlaced stalks of wheat creating beauty that no one suspected might be hidden inside a tree trunk brought from the dense thickets of the forest.

Bento was astonished by the discovery of the sculptor inside him. He spent hours dedicated to his craft — his art — following designs that he imagined first, then passed carefully onto paper and, little by little, created in relief on wood panels. He enjoyed mixing memories of Portugal with what he saw around him. When the priests asked him to evoke the sacrament of the bread and wine in his work, he brought them to the altar in an original way. Amid the thin stalks representing the wheat that they didn't have in Brazil, he sowed corn-cobs with their fat kernels. Nestled among the grapes that reminded him of the vineyards across the sea, he carved tropical berries, cashews and pineapples. And underneath the crowning garlands of roses and banana flowers, he set warblers and hummingbirds, with bear cubs and monkeys peeking out below.

The angels, however, were totally inspired by the inhabitants of the new land. Bento didn't sculpt images of chubby angels with wavy blond hair and fine tapered noses. Instead they always came out with prominent cheekbones, wide nostrils, tight curls like those of Africans, or smooth, long hair like the Indians. He had no other models. Almost all the children he saw around him had features of the Africa they had just left or the American forest they came from. Manuela was probably the only European under fifteen in the whole area. But she had grown so much that she could no longer be considered a child.

Fascinated by her brother's work, the girl often came to see the figures that were sprouting from the wood. They were beautiful.

"It makes me want to make something for the church, too," she said.

Dona Catarina liked the idea and began making lace for altar cloths with Manuela, Beatriz and Felipa. They spent hours engaged with threads wound on bobbins, working them over a pillow to make the lace. Manuela imagined that she was making a new set of clothes for Our Lady, bringing back memories of her mother and the beautiful Virgin who had protected her when she was alone during those cold nights in Lisbon, praying for Bento stuck in a dank, dark dungeon.

At some point during their flight and suffering, she had lost the rosary that belonged to her mother. But she didn't need to count beads in order to pray, nor did she need to use memorized or decorative language. She continued to talk with Our Lady silently, or to ask the spirits of her mother and father for protection.

She remembered the nights she had slept at the altar in the stone church. Those were difficult times. Now she was doing well in a new land, with Bento and surrounded by friends. She prayed for Dona Ines, Don Diogo and Don Gaspar in gratitude for helping her and her brother. If there were no slavery, with the brutal suffering it brought, she would have been completely happy. She prayed for freedom for Didi and his family, and for a world without captivity. She could never forget that everyone was a part of one big whole. Sometimes it seemed that her entire life was like the lacework she created with Beatriz, Felipa and Dona Catarina — full of interwoven threads forming new designs. It was just that the dangers that they were living through were not always as beautiful and delicate as the panels of altar cloth.

But soon Manu was full of other ideas. She liked to do lacework — yes — but she wanted to try something else. She had the idea of making ceramic candlesticks for the new altar. Dona Catarina admired the lively girl and let her find her own way. She allowed her to work alongside the Indian women, helping them collect the riverside clay they called tabatinga that they used to shape pots, pitchers, candlesticks and ornaments.

It was obvious that the girl was very happy taking up her father's craft and turning the wet clay into useful vessels. She dreamed of doing painted and glazed pottery, like the dove that still went everywhere with her. Perhaps she would start with white and blue or yellow tiles. But she knew nothing of pigments or high kiln temperatures. And the Indians didn't work in that way. They preferred to paint pottery with lines forming beautiful designs, but in only one color. In any case, Manuela loved being with the women, laughing and talking, cheerful and playful as they worked on the bowls, pitchers, jars and pots.

It was also a good thing that Antonio Caiubi had returned. In the exchange of groups between the Jesuit school and the village, it was once again his turn to be in Amparo. And she loved his company.

Now there were three friends. Everyone had a lot to do, and free time was scarce. But whenever they could be, Manu, Didi and Caiubi were together. Sometimes Beatriz and Felipa accompanied them. Other times, only the boys got together, while the girls were embroidering or making lace. The whole group would talk under the quitungo, fish, make traps to catch birds, pick fruit, bring in cassava from the fields, and braid fibers to make baskets or mats. Working together they got more done.

Manu, at least, usually found a way to escape and be close to one or both of the boys. Dona Catarina wasn't sure what to think of these friendships. Sometimes she was amused, but other times she was worried, feeling that Manuela should be acting more like a proper young woman. She was growing up, and so were Beatriz and Felipa. It wouldn't be long before it was time to think about marriage for the three of them. They weren't children any longer — they couldn't continue to go wherever they wanted with the boys. She even discussed the matter with Bento.

"She has always been this way, Senhora Catarina, since she was little. Perhaps it's because she was the only girl in a family with three boys. And then when it was just the two of us alone in the world, she was used to being near me. Don't worry, it's just the way Manu is."

Considering that Bento, the older brother who was responsible for the girl, didn't think there was anything wrong, the widow decided to drop the subject. But she didn't like to see Beatriz and Felipa always with the two boys and tried to keep them at home a little more.

The people of Amparo were used to seeing Manuela, Caiubi and Didi — so different yet so bonded to each other — going together from place to place. They were such a part of the landscape that they didn't really attract anyone's attention.

Little by little, Manuela and Didi were learning to appreciate Caiubi's knowledge. The Indian boy was able to find his way in the jungle as if he were on a familiar street, or even at home. He could identify edible fruits or roots, or plants that held water in their stems. He could shoot arrows with perfect marksmanship. He was aware of the sudden silence announcing the flight of a hawk overhead. He recognized animal tracks and the paths the animals chose. He knew where they were going to drink water and the burrows where they hid. He would notice treetops moving across the creek when there was no wind, and then draw his friends' attention to some monkeys playing.

Gradually, they talked about other matters, like quilombos. Antonio Caiubi knew several routes that might lead to them.

"Many of our braves know where they are. They help the escaped slaves find them. But no one must know that here in Amparo."

"You know where they are? You know how to get there?"

"I've never been, but some warriors in my village have. And I know of one, from another villager who moved there."

"Along with the runaways? Blacks and Indians?"

"Why not? That way they can all defend themselves better. Or have you forgotten that your people want to enslave us, too?"

Manu didn't need to respond. She knew that very well. And she knew the reason for Caiubi's repressed half smile when he added, "I mean, they would if they could …"

She had heard many stories of fierce struggles between the indigenous people and the whites who hunted them down. But she sometimes forgot that when she saw the Indian boys at the Jesuit school, or the Indian women making cassava flour in a quitungo or making baskets or pottery — in peace.

Didi returned to what interested him most. "Do you think you can find out where these routes are?"

Caiubi stayed silent for a while, his eyes downcast.

Before he answered, Manu added, "And help someone in the woods avoid danger and the poisonous beasts?"

More silence, more lowered eyes. The boy thought a lot about what he was going to say. Finally, he replied, "Alone, maybe not. But if there's time, I can prepare myself. And I can get help from my family and friends."

Looking Didi straight in the eye, he added decidedly, "I know what you're thinking. I'm your friend. You can count on me."

He would be a great support, Didi was sure.

"It will be our secret," Manu concluded. "You cannot talk about it with anyone."

They didn't need to hear this advice. All three of them knew the risk they were running.

In the months that followed, things changed very slowly. In the church of Amparo, Bento was gradually covering the bottom of the wooden altar with angels surrounded by ornaments of leaves, fruits, vegetables, birds and small animals. Clay animals and people were emerging from Manuela's hands, and it was clear that when Christmas came, there would be a nativity scene recreating the birth of the baby Jesus. Father Vicente had seen one in Italy and suggested that the girl make it. From Caiubi came more and more secrets of the forest and, finally, one surprising piece of information — the quilombos were communicating with each other. They soon might be able to find out which one Didi's father was in. The hope of seeing his father was gradually building Didi's determination to escape.

Before that day came, however, Bento managed to convince Quim that he had to go back to Amarante, and this time he should take someone to help him transport the heavy timbers he might need. He made up a story so compelling involving the furniture orders and the choice of trees to be felled that Senhora Catarina eventually agreed to allow Didi to accompany him.

And so the two went.

As they approached the stream that signaled they were nearing Amarante, Bento saw that the women were once again doing their hard work of washing clothes. He barely had time to speak.

"Didi, if you ever recognize anyone from your village, you have to be very smart and do as your father did with you on the beach that day. Don't let on. Don't give the owners any reason to be suspicious or let anyone think the meeting is strange. Make sure the foreman doesn't notice."

The boy didn't answer. He had stopped suddenly and was staring at the river's edge, at one of the slaves who had walked away a little from the group to hit a wet shirt against a rock.

"That's Rosa," Bento explained. "My friend."

"No," Didi corrected, trembling. "That's Danda. My sister."

"That's what I suspected. In fact I was almost certain, which is why I wanted to bring you here. But don't give anything away yet. We need to be careful. On second thought, I'm going to go and prepare her so she doesn't let on that she knows you."

While Didi waited on the hill with the mule, Bento went slowly down the slope. Once they saw him, the washerwomen stopped working and greeted him.

Some began exchanging glances and smiles, because they knew he would do just what he did — approach Rosa and start talking to her in a low voice.

But they couldn't have imagined what he was saying. They saw the girl put her hands to her chest, still holding a soaking shirt that was dripping all over her. The others laughed, thinking that she must be nervous to see Bento again. They didn't understand why Rosa laughed as the boy helped her collect the clothes she had dropped, her moist eyes fixed on the hilltop where a black boy was standing beside a mule.

"Don't let anyone suspect," Bento said to Rosa.

"But my mother will cry with joy. Everyone will know."

"Then we have to let her know ahead of time. It's very important."

"But how? You'll get to the house before I do and she'll see Odjidi."

"Yes, but I won't go inside. I'll ask permission to leave the mule tied to the corral and then go with the boy to take a peek in the woods, while it's still light. I'll say that I want to pick a good tree for Senhora Barbara's bed. That way he won't go to the kitchen porch immediately, and your mother won't see him."

"But …"

"Leave it to me to work out with Don Vasco and Senhora Barbara. I've thought of everything. You talk to your mother and prepare her. I'll come back tonight.

You and your mother can meet Didi at the fire in front of the slaves' quarters. It will be dark and there will be fewer people around. Then you can talk. But you must be discreet."

"Didi? Who is Didi?"

"Didi is your brother Odjidi."

And that is what they did.

And since Bento stayed over another day and night at the Amarante mill, there was an opportunity for more conversation. Although the other slaves thought Rosa and Chica were giving the boy a lot of attention, they were satisfied with the explanation that they recognized him as the son of a neighbor from their village. They didn't suspect the truth. They had no idea that he had brought them news of Guezo. That is, as much news as Bento felt he could give without jeopardizing anyone's safety.

Didi told them that he had seen his father from a distance, unloading the bullock cart, but that they hadn't been able to speak to each other. He said that the foreman was very violent, and that they had to be careful. His father was a slave at a plantation some leagues away, on the west side of the forest. And he had sent a message to his son saying he was fine.

All true. But incomplete.

Following Bento's advice, Didi didn't mention Guezo's escape or the quilombo. It was valuable but risky information, which could be dangerous if it fell on the wrong ears. They covered it up with a white lie, leaving some hope that perhaps Guezo would come to Amparo again or send news.

For his part, Bento advised Don Vasco and Senhora Barbara to use mahogany for the canopy bed. There were good trees in the woods, and they themselves could choose which ones to cut down. He gave them several possibilities — they could have just the bed or take the opportunity to order a pair of night tables and a clothes chest as well. The timber could be transported to Amparo, but in fact that wouldn't be necessary. Although the carpenters in Amarante were only used to manufacturing rough pieces, they were very good. They could get a start on the work, doing the heaviest parts of the job, and then he could come to guide them, while he was doing the drawings and fine finishes.

It seemed like a good idea, and so it was arranged.

18

―――

Dreams and Secrets

IN THE MIDST of hard work and various comings and goings between the village of Amparo and the Amarante mill, time passed.

In the village, Bento convinced the Jesuits that he needed some apprentices. Father Vicente chose three very skilled students to help him. Their assistance made it possible to finish the work on the church altar just in time for Christmas.

It was a beautiful celebration that lasted several days. For a few weeks, the Indian children had been rehearsing a play at the Jesuit school. The priests liked to organize a play for special occasions, and the Indians liked to participate. Everyone enjoyed the rehearsals and preparations. And on Christmas Eve, everyone — the people of Amparo and many from the surrounding mills like Amarante — could see and hear the result.

But the celebration involved much more. First, there was a procession. Then, in front of the church, everyone stopped to listen to the beautiful singing by a children's choir of hymns celebrating the coming of God to live among the people. Then a public ceremony recreated the birth of the baby Jesus, with all its stories. It showed the glory of Jesus, the angels, the guiding star, the adoration of the shepherds, the visit of the Three Kings. But it also showed the poverty in which Jesus decided to enter the world, the violence of the persecution by Herod, and Herod's massacre of the innocents.

It was only when the celebration outside was over that the doors of the church were opened and everyone entered to see the new altar and the ceramic nativity scene. They were dazzling.

The candlelight revealed the beauty of the wood carved by Bento with the help of Indians and slaves. The wood carvings stood out, rising behind the altar stone covered by the lacework made by Dona Catarina, Beatriz, Felipa and other women in the village. On the side, near the door that gave way to the cloister, was another attraction — a pretend grotto made of rough, dyed, crushed cloth that housed the clay figures made by Manuela and the Indian women. The nativity scene included the Holy Family, the Magi, the shepherds, the angels, as well as a host of other visitors and animals — dolls representing fishermen, basket weavers, porters, farmers, woodsmen, dogs, agoutis, coatis, parrots, frogs and alligators. They all came to celebrate the birth of Jesus.

It was beautiful. Everyone was delighted by the new altar and the nativity. Then the Christmas mass began. In his sermon, Father Braz spoke about the meaning of the coming of the Redeemer, the hope of humanity. But he also talked about the joy of everyone being assembled in peace that night, in a church that had become so beautiful and that owed so much to the work of an artist like Bento.

Hearing these words, the boy remembered the conversation he'd had with the priests a few days before. Father Vicente had said that he owed the beauty of the altar to Bento, and he didn't know how to pay him. The boy had drummed up his courage and answered in a straightforward way.

"I know how."

Curious, the priest asked, "Tell me. Is it something we can do?"

"I don't know. But I know what I would like. I want you to help me marry Rosa Chica."

Given the priest's surprise, he explained who Rosa was and how much the two of them liked each other. He didn't need to say anything about the difficulties of such a marriage, because they were obvious. She was a slave and had owners. No need to say more.

"I'll think about it. We will talk again tomorrow," promised Father Vicente.

The next day, Bento was called to have another conversation, this time with all the priests. They sympathized with his request, but had no idea what could be done to make it happen. They didn't have a plan, but they had some suggestions.

Some thought that first Rosa should be baptized. Others said that maybe Bento could work and save money to buy her and give her her freedom.

"Make money? How? Will the church pay me for my work? Or will Rosa's owners give me enough for the furniture that she could stay with me?"

There wasn't much money in the colony. Everyone knew that. Most of the time, payments were made through the exchange of goods. If a craftsman was dependent on making a lot of money to pay for something, it would take too long. Bento wasn't willing to wait. And the priests didn't have money to give him.

"We can give you two cows, or a cow and a mule. Maybe you can offer them in exchange for the slave?"

Bento scratched his head. Would Don Vasco be interested? Would it be enough? There was already a lot of livestock in Amarante.

"Or we can suggest that Don Vasco give you Rosa in exchange for the furniture."

"I would need to make furniture for many years, for many more people."

"But Dona Catarina would like a woman slave in exchange for the boy she has," said Father Braz. "She says she has more need of a woman inside the house than a boy who spends his time loitering in the streets. Maybe Didi could go to Amarante and Rosa could come here."

Bento hadn't thought of that. But he remembered Manu telling him that the boy had spent a long time trying to get Beatriz and Felipa to convince the widow that he could earn her something if she negotiated with Don Vasco. It was his way of trying to get closer to his mother and sister. More than that, it was part of his secret dream that one day he would flee with them to a quilombo. But he hadn't spoken about that with anyone except Manu and Caiubi.

In any case, it didn't make much difference to Bento if Rosa were a slave of Don Vasco or Dona Catarina. She would still be a slave. And he wanted something quite different — for her to be free and to be his wife.

But the priests' help was precious, and he knew it. And if they were going to give him two cows in payment, maybe he could trade them with Dona Caterina in exchange for Rosa. Or who knows? Maybe the deal would be complete with something else? A canoe, perhaps? That was something he could make himself. He'd choose a good tree in the woods and dig the trunk. Maybe the widow would be interested in having two cows in the yard, so that she could sell milk and make cheese. And a canoe that the fishermen could use and pay for with a fifth of what they earned, as was the custom. Maybe the priests could add some chickens to what they would pay Bento in exchange for the carved altar ...

In other words, the young carpenter's thoughts were far from the Christmas celebration and mass. He had his dreams and his secrets.

Beside him, Manuela had her own. She had already worked some things out with Caiubi, who had managed to bring them news of Guezo. They now knew which quilombo Didi's father was in. So they already had a destination for the family for when they escaped. The plans were beginning to come together. But she suspected that Bento had some ideas of his own about Rosa. She would need to talk to him, so that one plan didn't get in the way of the other.

Didi had also started to plan what he would do without being too sure of anything yet. As he listened to the choir sing, his thoughts wandered. The first thing to do was to keep going to the Amarante mill with Bento, so that one day he would have the chance to help his mother and sister escape. He realized he would need to convince Rosa, who resisted the idea of fleeing to the bush in the interior. He didn't know why. Maybe she was afraid. The girl also talked a lot about wanting to come to town, to Dona Catarina's house. The boy didn't understand how anyone could accept working for others as a slave when there was a chance to escape to the forest. Was it fear of Indians and wild animals? Manu thought that Rosa wanted to stay close to Bento. Maybe that was it. Sometimes girls understood these things better. If so, Didi would let Rosa do what she wanted. He would trade places with his sister, then. Beatriz and Felipa had almost convinced the widow to propose the exchange to the owners of Amarante.

And if he went to the Amarante mill, he had everything well thought out and resolved. To begin with, one day he would help his mother escape. He would find a way to make it look as though she had fallen into the river. She would wait in hiding until Caiubi picked her up. Then, at the first opportunity, he would go to her. And with the help of the warriors in Caiubi's tribe, they would run away together for the quilombo where Guezo was.

These were the dreams and secrets that the boy was thinking about as he stood near the door at the back of the church.

In the chorus, the voice of Antonio Caiubi mingled with the voices of other Indian boys and girls. He looked with pride at the nativity scene that his friend Manuela had taught the Indian women to make, and who in turn taught her to paint it with annatto and genipap. He was happy. He had good news to tell his friends when the mass was over. He had talked to his father when he was home. His father had agreed, when the time came, to go with a group of warriors to lead Didi and his family to Guezo's quilombo. Gradually, the plan was taking shape. The Indian boy would miss his black friend a lot when he was gone. But he couldn't help but feel happy for him. And he would always have his friendship with Manuela.

She was so pretty today, wearing a new Christmas dress, her hair braided and decorated with flowers. He was hoping she would like the gift he had made for her — a necklace of feathers and seeds, with all the colors of the forest. He wanted to take the girl to his village for a day. He was sure she'd love it. Maybe she could live there one season, sleeping in one of the hammocks that crisscrossed the hut and swimming in the river at dusk. If they got married one day, as he sometimes dreamed, would they live in Amparo or in the Indian village? It was still too early to know. But it was never too early to dream … until the day arrived.

Each one of them had their dreams and secrets tucked away. Some of these hidden thoughts may have gone up to heaven in the form of a prayer. Others may have glided up there with the sounds of the voices singing, so well rehearsed and so in harmony that they seemed like a heavenly choir. A chorus of angels with different features, just like the ones carved on the altar.

This Christmas Eve, it wasn't yet possible to know if these dreams would come true.

It was enough to feel that they would. And that was very good.

Editorial Note

MANU AND BENTO's story opens in Lisbon, Portugal, in the early 1600s, at a time when Portugal was ruled by Spain (1580–1640).

Across the ocean was the Portuguese colony of Brazil, where the Portuguese first arrived in 1500. In order to establish and settle themselves in the new land, the colonists were heavily dependent on slave labor — in the early years drawn from the indigenous population and, later, through the importation of African slaves. The numbers of African slaves brought to the colony began to swell in the 1580s with the growth of sugar cane plantations and the exportation of sugar to Europe.

In 1630, the Dutch, who were at war with Spain, invaded northeast Brazil, and stayed for almost thirty years. Following the invasion, the Portuguese army was focused more on fighting the Dutch than chasing runaway slaves, which enabled the existence and growth of quilombos — communities of fugitive slaves living in less accessible regions of the forest. Perhaps best known is the Palmares quilombo, which grew to a size of 20,000 inhabitants by the 1690s.

Slavery was finally abolished in Brazil in 1888.

Glossary

acacia A tree or shrub in the pea family, found in tropical climates, that is often thorny.

agouti A small rodent similar to a guinea pig but larger and with longer legs.

annatto A small evergreen tree or shrub. The red seeds are used to make body paint or dye.

Avanheém The language of the indigenous Tupi people, which was spoken as a common tongue in colonial Brazil; also known as Old Tupi.

baobab A long-lived tree, native to Africa, with a very thick trunk and edible fruit. It survives in drought by storing great quantities of water in its trunk.

brazilwood A heavy wood from tropical trees in the pea family that produces deep red dye.

cloister A covered, arched walkway, looking onto a courtyard on one side and having a wall on the other; usually part of a monastery or church.

coati A member of the raccoon family.

cumbuca A Portuguese word of Tupi or indigenous origin for a gourd-shaped bottle made of clay.

cunhã A Portuguese word of Tupi or indigenous origin for girl.

curumim A Portuguese word of Tupi or indigenous origin for boy.

genipap A tree found in the American tropics that produces edible fruit, which is also used to make blue dye.

Hail Mary A traditional Christian prayer to Mary, the mother of Jesus, who is also known as the Holy Virgin.

Inquisition A religious court of the Roman Catholic Church that sought out and harshly punished non-believers. The Portuguese Inquisition, starting in 1536 and lasting until 1821, targeted converts from Judaism and Islam.

league A measure of distance by land, roughly equivalent to 3 miles (4.8 km).

mahogany A tree found in the American tropics that has hard, reddish-brown wood, often used in making furniture.

moringa A Portuguese word of African origin for a clay jar used to keep drinking water cool.

nave The main interior part of a Christian church, from the entrance to the altar.

petrel A seabird.

pulpit A raised area or platform where a priest or minister stands to give a sermon or lead the service.

quilombo A Portuguese word of African origin for a community or settlement of runaway slaves in remote areas of colonial Brazil.

quitungo A Portuguese word of African origin for an open-air straw hut used by fishermen.

refectory The dining room in a school or monastery.

sacristy A room in a church where the priest keeps robes and sacred vessels, and prepares for the service.

sexton A person who takes care of a church and its surroundings.

shrine Also known as an oratorio in Brazil — a small wooden structure, often in the shape of a miniature chapel, with doors that open to reveal the image of a saint or saints.

sibipuruna A Portuguese word of Tupi or indigenous origin for a large evergreen tree, native to Brazil.

tabatinga A Portuguese word of Tupi or indigenous origin for clay found on the riverbank in Brazil.